I0665246

THE UPSHOT

by

Brad Spencer

ASKME Publishing

Chicago

Copyright C. 2014 by Brad Spencer (BradSpencer.net)

All rights reserved.

ISBN: 978-0692220412

ISBN 13: 0692220410

ASKME Publishing, Chicago

Acknowledgements

This book could not have been completed without the support of so many people, but the five I want to thank the most are Eileen, Abigail, Sarah, Kate and Marie. I am blessed to have you all in my life. Also a special thanks to family and friends for their direct and indirect encouragement of the writing of this book. You know who you are. Or maybe you don't...yet.

For Lost Souls

1

A Little Peace

It's been nearly a year since the tragic ordeal finally had somewhat of a resolution.

I still think about it, nearly every day, but not all of it. Not everything. That one night twenty-five years or so ago, the one when it all began, changed my life forever, probably made me bitter about the world, skeptical of people, timid, and weak. Time made it worse, as I know it did for her. She was never the same. How could she be? If it had never happened, she might have gone down a better path. I take that back. I know she would have done something with her life. She was intelligent, confident, and beautiful. Everything was there for a life worth living.

If it had never happened, I'm certain we all would have gone down better paths.

For years after that night I used to try to make myself feel better by repeating over and over again that there was nothing that could be done about it, but I would never convince myself. It was selfish and ignorant thinking, I know now. As the years dragged on, the torment compounded. I'd be alone, and a sad song from that time would summon the memory. And, man, my soul would go dark, and I'd be angry at him and at her but angrier at myself. I'd weep uncontrollably—not softly but frantically. I'd want to burst with fury. I'd imagine myself seeing him some place and waiting until he was walking home, maybe through a dark alley at night. It would be raining, and I'd step out of the shadows and say, "Do you remember me?" He wouldn't answer, and I'd say something cheesy like, "Well, you're going to remember this!" And I'd punch him square in the jaw. He'd fall, and I'd pounce on his chest, pin him down with my knees, and then pound my fists into his face and release all that fury. Get it all out. All for her. All for us. All for humanity. All for truth.

Yes, I remember. Back then I'd imagine killing him to save her, to save us, to save the world. But that was back when I only fantasized about it. Those images now just clash with actual memories, the memories that fill out our history. Twenty-five years of fantasies mixed with what actually happened a year or so ago.

I used to wonder what he was thinking that night. I wondered what I was thinking. I wondered what she was thinking. What would have become of our lives had we done something about it? Maybe Holly Karlan wouldn't have ended up as she had, so self-destructive. Maybe I wouldn't have been so sufferable. Maybe my best friend, Jimmer Cuddy, wouldn't have become so…disturbed.

Maybe the three of us would be together.

Maybe I wouldn't be living with yet another profound secret.

For years, Cuddy and I endured the heaviest of guilt, while Holly suffered a pain unimaginable. Back then I racked my brain every dark day, feverishly searching for a way to make what happened to her right, sometimes even considering just going to the police and telling them what I knew. After moving nearly two thousand miles away, after struggling through college, after pinning down a job, after marriage, after a kid, I couldn't shake what happened that night. I thought about going through the background check and the waiting period, getting a permit, and legally purchasing a gun, finding him, shooting him dead, and simply accepting the consequences. It wouldn't change the past, but maybe it would close the gaping void in my conscience. But then it would hit me, the rationale. My family would suffer the consequences of my actions. I'd be ruining lives the way Rory James ruined lives.

And then somehow, almost miraculously, a year or so after she died, a year or so after Cuddy and I stood atop this rock overlooking the valley near where we grew up and believed there was no way to make things right, a window opened. And my best friend, who had killed before, was willing to kill again. We could make it right with no consequences, maybe finally find some solace in our lives.

But I guess fate again stepped in the way.

No, I don't like to think about the way it all ended. Maybe because it will never end until I'm gone.

See, I believe that the only thing the three of us ever wanted out of our lives was a little peace. I hope my friends Jimmer Cuddy and Holly Karlan have their peace. I live for them. And I think that's why I'm back up on this rock, in this agonizing heat, overlooking the vast valley of this beautiful but complicated state, in this celebrated but vulnerable country, in this marvelous but troubled world, where the good try to survive among the evil day and night. Yes, I'm going to go on living for them until my time is up.

And may the three of us be together again someday, if the fates allow.

2

If the Fates Allow

S top shoving me, Jimmer! Ms. Berry is gonna get mad and not let us sing and my parents are here…I think."

Sam squinted and shaded the lights over the stage with his hand. Peering out at the audience, he tried to spot his parents among the throng of adults bustling about, looking for empty or unsaved seats.

While Sam's arm was up, Jimmer jumped and shoved a finger into his armpit.

"Ouch! You pee-head!" Sam socked him on the arm, and they both giggled. Just then Ms. Berry gave them a stern look and nodded at the girl in dark pigtails to Jimmer's left.

"You guys are so weird," said Holly as she shuffled between them, her dark pigtails swaying, the sequins on her red dress sparkling in the lights in the same fashion as her crisp blue eyes. "Oh look, there's my mommy and daddy! Wave, you guys!"

The three of them straightened up, smiled, and waved to Holly Karlan's parents, who were sitting near the back row, the both of them waving back frantically, Holly's father also trying to film the moment with his video camera. Jimmer stopped waving, leaned behind Holly, grabbed Sam's shirt, and pulled him back until he fell on his butt.

"These are new corduroys!" squealed Sam.

Jimmer mimicked him in a high-pitched voice. "These are new corduroys! Sorry, Sammy Mac!" He giggled and turned away as Holly helped Sam up.

"I'm gonna flick a booger on you later, Jimmer," Sam grumbled, "when you're not lookin!"

"Shush!" Ms. Berry was growing impatient.

The music teacher, Mr. Howell, stepped up to the front of the stage, nervously scratched his salty beard, and adjusted his striped tie.

"Ladies and gentlemen, welcome to Cochise Elementary School's holiday sing-along recital. We're glad you're all here, and we hope you enjoy our little presentation that the kids have worked so hard on the last few weeks. We're beginning with Ms. Berry's first-grade class."

He raised his arm with a flourish, and the audience began to applaud. He walked to a small piano and sat. With a nod he began to play, and the children began to sing. They sang "Jingle Bells" first, and then "Feliz Navidad," and then "Santa Claus is Coming to Town." A few of the kids in front used tambourines and xylophones to create a rhythm.

Sam spotted his parents and waved. Jimmer saw him waving and mimicked it.

After a few more songs, Mr. Howell stood up and faced the small crowd. "Ms. Berry's class will now finish its portion of the show with the sweet little holiday song, 'Have Yourself a Merry Little Christmas.'"

The audience applauded, and Mr. Howell sat back down at the piano and began to play.

As he sang, Jimmer reached around Holly and tried to pinch Sam on the elbow. Sam knocked his arm away and shook his head. Jimmer tried again, and again Sam knocked it away and put his finger to his nose threatening to pick it and fling something toward his friend. Jimmer looked at Holly, who was singing and paying attention to Mr. Howell and the audience, and began mimicking her dramatically. Playfully, she shoved him and told him to stop.

"Have yourself a merry little turkey sandwich," belted Jimmer, causing both Holly and Sam to giggle incessantly. But then Holly gathered herself and took hold of the boys' hands.

Sam looked down, surprised. Gently, she squeezed, and he squeezed back. Jimmer looked down and then back up at Holly, who turned to him and smiled. He smiled back, and they finished singing the song.

Faithful friends who are dear to us
Gather near to us once more

Every kid in Ms. Berry's class was singing except one, the tall kid standing in the middle of the group. He looked bored and kept jerking his head up to keep his thick brown bangs from falling into his brown eyes.

Ms. Berry squeezed her plump torso between the rows. "Rory!" she whispered harshly. "Rory James! Why aren't you singing?"

He shrugged and then seemed to fixate on the three kids standing on a lower riser in front of him. They were holding hands. He looked around to see if any of the other kids were holding hands. None were.

Mr. Howell hadn't said anything to us about holding hands, had he?

A sad look washed over his face. He reached out to the girl next to him and tried to take her hand, but she brushed him off. He tried again, and she looked at him quizzically and pushed his hand away.

Rory James grabbed the girl's hand forcefully and held it tight. She shot him an angry look but kept on singing. He grinned.

As the other kids continued to sing, Rory James stood there motionless, not sure what it was he was feeling, squeezing the girl's hand tighter and tighter and staring at three of his classmates in front of him.

Sam, Holly, and Jimmer continued to hold hands and sing:

Through the years we all will be together
If the fates allow...

3

Holly

As a young girl, Holly Karlan was the whole package: Pretty, smart, and funny. Dark hair, blue eyes, inquisitive mind. She was athletic and graceful, tough and sensitive. She was clever, knew more about people and their ways than she let on. When she was five years old, she would race Jimmer and Sam up and down the street on her bike, taking a prominent lead but easing up near the end and letting one of them win. She knew they'd sulk and go home if she won. She'd feign disappointment and grin wryly underneath her look of frustration as the boys celebrated their victory.

Her mother was a stay-at-home and her father an always-cordial and always-portly loan officer at a local bank. Conservative Republicans. She had no siblings.

The family, Catholic, went to church every Sunday morning. Her mother volunteered for Girl Scout events, and her father helped coach T-ball and soccer. They never missed a block party and usually hosted at least one dinner a year with neighbors.

At a young age, Holly was never a troublemaker, never a drama queen, never a diva. Temper tantrums were something other kids did. She helped around the house, did her homework without being told, and watched television with her parents. When she grew up she wanted to be a veterinarian, a horse trainer, a mom, a princess, a schoolteacher, a banker, a baker, the president, and a wife.

At nine years old, she told her mom she was the most influential person in her life. Her mom was flattered. "Well, I couldn't have asked for a better daughter. You are the best thing that ever happened to me and your father. I love you so much, Holly."

At twelve years old, Holly told her father she someday hoped to marry a guy just like him and have children. He was flattered. "You make sure he treats you right, Holly, before you say yes. You deserve a real special guy."

At fifteen years old, she told them both they were the best parents in the world and how much she appreciated everything they did for her and would do for her in the future. "Well, we're just so proud of you with all your schoolwork and your positive attitude and the way you go out of your way to be friendly and to help others. You're truly a wonderful kid, Holly."

At eighteen years old, she told them to go fuck themselves and die. She didn't care what she was doing to herself or with her life. They didn't understand her. They didn't really know her.

"Holly! Don't talk like that. You don't know what you're saying," begged her mother.

Tattoo. Nose ring. Therapy. More tattoos. "What curfew? I'm not drunk! I'm shit-faced wasted!"

Gasp, "Holly! How dare you?"

"Fuck you. Fuck all of you. Fuck everyone. I'm so out of here. I don't need college. I don't need you!"

Alcohol. Marijuana. Heroin. Cocaine. Heroin plus cocaine equals speedball. Overdose. Drug rehab. Heroin. Heroin. Heroin. Drug rehab. Heroin.

One afternoon, when Holly was supposed to be attending one of her courses at a nearby junior college, and her mother was supposed to be at her spinning class, her mother walked in on Holly and a girl and a boy she didn't recognize having sex in her mother's bed. All three of them, naked, wrapped up, a blanket of skin.

"That's it! Get out! Get out, you ungrateful little bitch! I don't ever want to see your face again! Get out! Get the *eff* out of my house and take these…these filthy, disgusting people with you!"

Later that night, her mother, bawling her eyes out, asked no one in particular, "What happened to my little girl?"

For some reason, Holly's father answered, "You coddled her too much. Now she's acting out."

"Oh shut up, Frank, you never disciplined her. She was always Daddy's little girl. Now she thinks she can get away with anything."

Soon after that, Holly's parents divorced, and the house was sold.

***

"I'm going to marry you, Sam McElroy," little Holly Karlan held up the picture-perfect female doll next to the picture-perfect male doll. "We will have children and a nice house, and we will be happy forever. We will live next to Jimmer and our parents, and I will be a teacher, and you will be a...a fireman. And our kids will be named Lucy and Beau, and we will have a dog named Zoey and a hamster named Gigi and no cats, because we both hate cats. We will have horse stables somewhere, and we will take our kids out to them and ride horses in the desert on trails up hills and through mountains. I will ride a mare, and you will ride a gelding, and Lucy will ride a filly, and Beau will ride a colt." Holly stopped and looked about her room.

"Mom! Where are my horses?"

"Check in the TV room on the couch, dear. Oh, and dinner is ready."

Holly frowned. She held up the dolls again. In a deep voice she said, "Holly Karlan, will you marry me?"

She turned her eyes on the female doll. "Yes, of course, Sam McElroy, I will marry you," she said in a soft voice. "But first I need to eat dinner."

4

J. Cuddy

The phone buzzed. J. Cuddy, irritated, answered it.
"What."

"Hey, it's me."

"Yeah, I know. What do you want?"

"We need to talk."

"Well, start talking then." Cuddy stoked the bowl of a small pipe with a lighter and took a hit. Paused. While exhaling, he added, "Why-aren't-you-talking-yet?" spitting out each word low and slow as the smoke filled the room.

Sam hesitated. His friend was acting strange. "I have a…"

"Hello? What's up, Sam Misery McElroy?"

"Why are you being such an asshole?"

Lighting a cigarette, Cuddy replied, "You're still miserable, and you want to know why? Because you're still calling me and not asking, 'How you doin, Cuddy, you doin good?' No, you just call up and start in with the same ole shit."

"How are you doing, Cuddy, you doing good?"

"Fuck you!"

I don't know what this guy wants, Sam said to himself. "Hey, something has come up. I have something, something...but I really don't want to talk over the phone. We need to talk face-to-face."

"Is it venereal warts? Because I hear there's a cream for that."

"C'mon, Cuddy, what's wrong with you, man? I've got my hands on something—"

"Is it your dick?"

"Would you be serious for one minute? It's something that could maybe change things."

"Nothin will change anything, nothin we do in the present or the future can change the past. The past is there, frozen in time. History. It cannot be changed. You need to accept that."

"You're high, aren't you? Still getting stoned at your age? You know, you didn't say that last year. You told me you wanted to...Remember what you said after her funeral?"

There was a long, silent pause.

"You're the one who convinced me otherwise, asshole. But I'm listening."

"I've changed my mind."

Another long, silent pause.

"Then you better come down here, because I ain't goin up there. I'm certain your bitch of a wife don't want me in the house, anyway."

"I'm going to try to convince Rachel that I'm coming down for a long weekend to catch a Sun Devils game or something with you and the guys."

"Good luck with that. And if that doesn't work?"

"Then I'll tell her you're messed up again, and I need to come bail you out…I don't know."

"Goodbye, fuck-face."

J. Cuddy put down the phone and lifted himself up from the couch. He scratched himself through his sweatpants and walked over to a mirror hanging on the wall. Staring at his massive naked chest, he flexed, but he wasn't as proud as he had been of his physique in the past. The Marine emblem tat with the words "Semper Fi" stenciled beneath it on his left forearm tightened in a sinew of veins. The naked woman with the oversize tits and the long black hair riding a motorcycle on the other forearm did the same. He looked down at the red scar streaking across the woman and shook his head. Grinning, he pondered for a moment if that dumb *mujado* ever got those gold tooth caps out of his lung.

The large tats of machine gears on his left pectoral started up, first slowly and then churning aggressively. Cuddy always envisioned those gears grinding before he did his workouts, even the warm-ups to the warm-ups of his workouts. He turned around to check his deltoids, another red scar across his back tightening. When he finished flexing, he dropped down to the floor and began to do push-ups. He stopped after one hundred, stood back up, and went over to the kitchen table to a prescription bottle. He stood there for a moment staring at it. He shook the bottle, hearing the sound of the pills rattle inside. He turned and tossed them in the trash and went back to doing push-ups.

***

J. Cuddy wasn't always built like a brick house. He wasn't always so cross and short-tempered while teetering on the brink of manic-depression. He didn't always have scars on his face and a nasty one that resembled a slash across his back. In high school, he was small, thin, with a little boy's pale face. Back then, he was little Jimmer Cuddy. He looked as if he should have still been in middle school. But he was sweet to the girls, and his blue eyes and blond hair made up for his diminutive frame. The girls liked him, but only in a little brother sort of way. "Jimmer, you shouldn't be smoking that weed, give it to me." The girls would smoke the joint dry and then start making out with the guy sitting next to little Jimmer, the bigger guy. For some reason, Jimmer wouldn't protest. He wouldn't get pissed off. But that was before.

His short fuse, his temper, his overall curt, abusive, volatile disposition, his roller-coaster maniacal mood swings came on shortly after high school. Shortly after his father came home from his construction job, took his nine millimeter Berretta out of the dresser drawer, sat down at the end of the bed, and shot himself in the head. Jimmer had found him, blood oozing from his right temple. The old man was in debt, had just been pulled off yet another jobsite for losing his cool with a coworker. He had been pushed over the edge, apparently. Jimmer was devastated by the death itself, not so much that his father was dead, gone. His father rarely spoke to him anyway, rarely acknowledged that Jimmer existed at all. His father seemed always removed from everything, a ghost in the house.

Jimmer stayed in touch with the high school football coach, Coach Drago, short for Dominic Dragovic, an

Austrian Mr. Universe type, ripped from head to toe. And Drago took little Jimmer under his wing and got him working out. He was the guy who also supplied him with anabolic steroids, the premier drug at the time to turn a small bony kid into the Hulk—minus the green skin and the limited vocabulary. The drugs sure swelled Jimmer, and before long he was benching three hundred, squatting four hundred, deadlifting five hundred, and beating the shit out of guys who may or may not have crossed him. He was no longer little Jimmer, but J. Cuddy, and it was time to join the Marines.

It was his temper that got Corporal Cuddy dishonorably kicked out of the armed forces shortly after seeing combat in the Gulf War. It was during that time when he first went bonkers, ape-shit. At first, he was perfect for the military—fearless and eager to blow the shit out of anything or anyone he could. He took to the guns and to the training, but he never took to being told what to do and when to do it. He never fell for the honor of the uniform, didn't care, just wanted to hurt, maim, kill. The worst part was being away from his steroids. His 'roids were salvation for him. Those and the fierce workout regiments set the memory of what happened to his father and a friend of his aside and masked any guilt.

He was promoted to corporal early for being such a rigid nut, a devoted jarhead, but most of his comrades figured the brass did it just to try to settle him down.

He was an egomaniac, the self-described best at everything. He was foaming at the mouth when he arrived in Saudi Arabia, as hard as a cannon. But early in the fight, Corporal Cuddy and his fire team were among a convoy of LAVs (light armored vehicles) attacking a company of Iraqi tanks near the town of Al Khafji when the sky opened up on them and tore the hell out of everything. Cuddy lost all three men on his team, their body parts scattered across a desert field. Eleven US soldiers died during that fight. How he survived with a graze wound across his back was nothing short of a miracle. When he found out it was a US Air Force A-10 aircraft that did the hammering, he broke the nose of an orderly attending to his bandages, nearly choked to death his commanding officer, and tried to drive a Humvee into the arms depot.

While scud missiles were getting blown out of the night sky by patriot missiles and the US ground effort to push the Iraqi Army out of Kuwait was officially getting underway, Corporal Cuddy was on his way home.

Hey, it was better than a court martial. So long, Cuddy.

"So long, you fuckin grunts."

***

As time went on and the demand became greater, but the testing became more stringent, J. Cuddy and his mentor, Coach Drago, graduated from selling steroids to selling the next best thing, PEDs, performance enhancing drugs, clinically proven to make you a better man physically, a better athlete, a better anything you wanted to be. They also sold PED accessories in the form of deer-antler spray, flaxseed oil, the assorted creams, bogus vitamins, and, of course, syringes. They also sold the ubiquitous muscle-building "natural" pills and powdered shakes as supplements to the more popular illegal products.

Cuddy was quite popular at the fitness gyms in and around the valley. He loved sending the attractive housewives up the climbing wall, watching their toned asses jet out from the wall and their fake tits rub up against the handholds.

Not only was he a personal trainer to the many wealthy men and women living in the Phoenix area, but he was also one of Coach Drago's best salesmen, supplying the young twenty-somethings and teenagers looking to either recover snap-fast from an injury—HGH, baby, got it in a cooler in my jeep!—or to gain extra strength and quickness for an upcoming game—PEDs, get them while they're hot.

The market flourished. But then, with the multiple scandals at the professional sports levels, it began to slowly peter out. Coach Drago's lucrative business was forced to hawk other products, some that succeeded, some that didn't.

Cuddy had made a decent living selling for Coach. He lived in a two-level townhouse on a golf course near Camelback Mountain, which he hiked frequently—usually while popping his unsold amphetamines. Sometimes he'd sit atop the rock called the Praying Monk for hours at a time, thinking about his father, but mostly thinking about Holly Karlan, his lifelong friend.

He'd also think about a scumbag named Rory James.

5

El Diablo

Y ou'll call me?"

"I've got a few trips here and there, but I'll be in touch. It was a great night. You were fantastic. By far, the best I've ever had. You're special. I want you to know that. Special."

"Yeah, I guess it was a great night..." She looked down at the Gucci handbag and her clothes, and then at the bruises around her wrists, "a really fun, crazy, wild night." She looked back up at him curiously.

The woman, in her mid-twenties, brunette, mocha skin, long legs, large firm fake breasts, sauntered out of the portico of the adobe mansion, waving playfully but with a hint of suspicion at the guy standing in a black silk robe at the big oak door. She massaged her sore wrists and peered down in confusion at her ankles. They were tender and ringed in red. She noticed the bruises when putting on her shoes, but figured it was due to partying in high heels. Her shoulders ached, too. And her vagina felt bruised.

In the new Gucci handbag she had just received was her dress, bra, thong from last night, a hundred dollars cash for the cab ride home, and an assortment of jewelry and feminine products. She walked to the waiting cab in black skin-tight sweat pants and a pink sweat shirt that read "Pink Princess." Rory James watched her ass as she walked. He loved this part, seeing the monogramed letter R on one ass cheek and the letter J on the other. Perfect fit.

"You're a special girl!" he said, but when she went to turn to look at him and maybe wave goodbye, he had already closed the big oak door.

***

Rory James was a forty-three-year-old self-described venture capitalist. Home was in one of those adobe mountainside mansions well above the valley, complete with swimming pool, hot tub, guest house, five bed-rooms, five bathrooms, chef's kitchen, game room, and a six-car garage stocked with black Cadillac Escalade, sil-ver Mercedes S500, red convertible Porsche Boxter, souped-up brown Jeep Rubicon, teal Ferrari F430 Spider, two BMW K 1200 S motorcycles—one red, one blue—an assortment of dirt bikes, and other expensive toys. A private rattlesnake drive led up to the mansion, to a por-tico, to a turnaround complete with flowing fountain in the center. Not another mansion or conventional home for miles.

Yes, Rory James. An enormous framed portrait of himself hung over a marble fireplace in the living room. It was a portrait of him wearing a baseball uniform, standing on a mound, staring down a batter, ready to begin his windup. A close-up, his eyes tense, mouth clenched. He was young, handsome, and intently in the moment.

In the master suite were two walk-in closets, one full of expensive suits and designer clothes, the other full of female sleep wear, bikinis, shoes, silk robes, leggings, hairstyling products, expensive jewelry, cosmetic essentials, and anything else she may have needed to get out the door the next morning, including plenty of those Gucci handbags—gift bags, if you will.

This walk-in closet was also equipped with a hidden door in the back, behind it a dimly lit room fully stocked with black leather whips, ropes, steel chains, handcuffs, stiletto heels, thigh-high black leather boots, leather lingerie, leather riding crops, leather corsets, leather chaps, leather catsuits, leather and spiked dog collars, twisted nipplers, clit suckers, rubber cock ring harnesses, ring gag nipple clamps, hog-tie kits, and an assortment of strap-ons, some small, some obtrusively large.

Rory and his crew, his entourage, lived in the mansion.

His line of work?

When he was much younger Rory James was a super-athlete. He played all three major sports: football, basketball, and baseball. In high school, he starred in all three, excelled at all three. Senior year of high school, the lefty had a blazing fastball. Clocked at 99 mph. Drafted by the New York Mets. Signing bonus: a cool $2.4 million. A few years in the minors, arm goes limp. A couple of signings here and there to try to revitalize that arm didn't do anything but make that arm more rubbery. Still, good money. And then out of baseball.

But no matter, some "liaison consulting work" and a medium-size drug business netted big money for Rory. In the beginning, he was all about connecting the right people—athletes, athletic trainers, strength and conditioning coaches—to an old acquaintance, the same man who helped turn his 88 mph fastball into that 99 mph fastball by the use of…let's just say genetic engineering.

As time went on, it was persuasively recommended by his Mexican pharmaceutical supplier that he upgrade his portfolio to include heroin, coke, and meth. No problem. He also more than dabbled in chemistry, formulating his own narcotic concoctions, something he had a profound passion for.

Yes, Rory also ran a low-scale illegal narcotics business. And with the help of a dutifully crafty financial adviser, he banked a good buck.

So no, Rory James never held a real job, at least not a legitimate one. He was once an athlete and then an entrepreneur with a creative sense, but he was never truly satisfied with anything. He wanted more.

***

"Oh man, she has no idea the crazy stuff that happened last night!" The home echoed it back.

His crew, Tyler "T-Ray" Thompson, Herman "Hermie" Cortez, and Dale "Hosk" Hoskins, made their way from the game room to the expansive living room. All three men were roosters compared to Rory, either too chubby (T-Ray), too slim (Cortez), or too dumb (Hosk). Rory was fit, trim, and somewhat intelligent, because running even a low-scale illegal narcotics operation calls for at least some brains.

Rory had thick brown hair, acorn eyes and smooth tawny skin. The years hadn't done much to age the handsomeness out of the kid with the blazing fastball.

"Some wild night, RJ! I mean, we've had some wild nights, but that one by far was the wildest!" hollered Hosk, smiling giddily, waiting for Rory's—his boss's—confirmation. "She suspect anything?"

"Hell no, Hosk. Gas up the dirt bikes. T-Ray, load the guns. Let's go ride some bikes and shoot some shit!"

Just as the boys sat on the leather couches they bounded back up again, on their way to the garage to prepare for an afternoon of speed and adrenaline.

Rory James went straight to the master suite. When he reached the entrance, he turned around and called out, "Cortez!"

"Yes, boss," Herman Cortez answered from across the mansion. He came scurrying up the stairs and down the hall.

"Get in here. I need a shave."

Standing in the entrance of the luxurious bedroom, Rory James looked up at the beam in the middle of the ceiling.

Good, the boys put all the contraptions away.

Remembering the brunette hanging motionless over the bed the night before, his mouth widened into a wicked pirate smile.

"We've come a long way since the days of ecstasy," he said as Cortez walked in carrying a razor and shaving cream, a look of revulsion on his face.

***

Rory brought his motorbike to a skid, throwing dust up. He jumped off and swung the large tote bag off his back. His buddies came zipping across the arroyo off in the distance behind him, the sun gleaming off the visors of their helmets.

He took the Bushmaster Carbine M4A3 assault rifle out of the tote bag, switched off the safety, pursed his lips, hollered, "SAY HELLO TO MY LITTLE FRIEND," and blew the limbs off the jumping chollas scattered along a rock face.

"Fuck yeah!"

Cortez rode up and jumped off his bike. He was carrying another bag, this one with a watermelon, a few empty beer bottles, a cantaloupe, and other items to be used as targets. Rory tossed the Bushmaster to Cortez and retrieved a Glock from the tote bag. The other guys rode up on their bikes and stopped.

"Hey, Hermie, take that watermelon up to that rock," Rory commanded.

Reluctantly, Cortez put down the Bushmaster and picked up the watermelon. He made his way up and through the rock formations, dodging the chollas along the way. He wanted to set the watermelon down and move through the narrow passage as fast as possible. He began to worry.

Being out front of the boss while he's got a gun in his hand is dangerous. He's unpredictable at times, a loose cannon. One minute showerin you with praise, the next tellin you you're a piece of shit that doesn't deserve to be livin in such luxury and being paid to do it. Hosk probably wasn't lyin when he said boss shot a guy's thumb off once.

Cortez steadied the watermelon on an edgy rock and started to move down the slope.

"No, Hermie! Take it and hold it up!"

"Fuck," Cortez said quietly to himself. He walked back to the watermelon on the rock, muttering, "Holy hell, Herman Cortez, the shit you do for this psicópata. Trips down to Caborca to buy the merchandise, slippin stuff into the drinks of putas at the clubs, usherin them into his room, hearing the sounds, the loud music, the flashing lights in there—the guy is loco. He tie them up in there, hombre, the nasty shit he do to them, and you help him by settin all of it up. You jes as loco. Someday, someday one of the putas gonna go to the cops. Is all this worth it? You could go back to the sweat and grime yard work, get a little apartamento like the one you had."

He hefted the watermelon up over his head, hesitantly turned around, and closed his eyes. His black goatee beard beaded with sweat.

Rory belted out a sinister laugh, which T-Ray and Hosk echoed without really knowing why.

"Don't shit yerself, Hermie!"

Nervously, the guys laughed again.

The crisp pop echoed off the rocks, the wiz, and the slush.

Slowly, Cortez opened his eyes to see the desert, the trails, the dried-up riverbed, the face of a mountain not too far off in the distance, the sun bright and hot, and the blue sky.

"Gracias a dios!"

"Nice shot, boss," applauded T-Ray while reaching for another rifle in the tote bag.

"Yeah, gimme the shotgun now," said Rory.

T-Ray hesitated. Menacingly, Rory was looking up at Cortez in front of the rock.

"Boss, really? The shotgun? You might—"

Rory didn't ask again, just reached for the gun, a 12-gauge. He pumped it, "Not so fast, Hermie! Stay still!" He aimed.

Cortez's eyes widened, his face tightened up. He squinted into the sun, "Is that the shotgun?"

The watermelon exploded as Cortez let out a screeching cry, frantically checking his hands and his fingers. The red. The juice. No blood. He bent over shaking, breathing hard, trying to slow himself.

The sinister laugh made its way up the rock formation.

"Hey, Hermie, on your next trip to Caborca, purchase some of those military grade M27s so we can really have some fun out here."

"El diablo," muttered Cortez.

6

Sam McElroy

S am!"

"Yeah, honey, upstairs."

"You need to pick up Elsa from school today. Don't be late this time. I don't want the school calling me at work, it looks bad. My boss will think I've got an idiot for a husband..." Her voice trailed off as if she didn't really want him to hear the end of the statement.

"Yeah, no problem. Hey, honey, before you go, I want to run something by you."

Sam hopped down the stairs, then slowed in order not to come off too enthusiastic. "Hey, uh, Peter and Mike were talkin about wanting to take a roadtrip out to Arizona to see a game in a couple of weeks, and I mentioned I still have friends out there and a buddy where we could stay." He lifted his shoulders and scrunched his face to show he could go either way, yay or nay. No big deal.

"Two things," replied Rachel, holding up two fingers. "One, you've been down there a few times now in the last few years, so what's the story with that? And driving or flying? And don't tell me the so-called 'buddy' in Arizona you may or may not be staying with is that freak, J. Cuddy, you knew from high school."

"Yeah, probably drive. Cheaper," he replied, pretending to mull it over. "Probably drive, I'd probably drive, you know, because Pete's got just the one car, and Mike, well, you know how Mike's a cheapskate. Oh and...uh, Cuddy is actually that freak I've known my whole life, not just from high school, so, yeah, I was thinking we'd stay with him, save a little bit more money."

"You just saw him last year, flew down there for something."

Sam sighed. "I flew down there for a funeral, a girl we grew up with."

Rachel shrugged. "Whatever, go. I don't care."

He could sense the derision in her tone. "I'm sorry, did I say or do something to piss you off?"

"Honey, don't get your panties in a bunch," she replied. "Yes, I'll allow it. I can take Elsa to my mother's and maybe have a spa weekend."

The kiss barely touched Sam's cheek. Rachel was out the door. He hurried to grab his coat and followed. They would both leave for the train into Chicago at the same time every day, Sam off to his business-to-business writing job in an old and unkempt building in the West Loop and Rachel off to her high-profile digital marketing job in an upscale skyrise in the South Loop. But it was as if they didn't walk to the train stop together. She was always one step ahead. He followed like a lost puppy.

***

It was last year when I got the call, late at night, or more like early morning. With the phone ringing at such an hour, that feeling of dread falls over you. Same thing would happen if it was the doorbell late at night. Loud noises in darkness, that'll get your attention quick. I knew it was bad, just didn't know how bad or who was involved.

Rachel: "Jesus, who the hell is calling you this late?"

The area code was Arizona, the state I grew up in, lived there until I was out of high school, then moved up north to Illinois to go to college at Loyola, where I met Rachel. It wasn't my folks on the line, because they had left the desert long ago for the sunny beaches of Florida. It was either Cuddy or a wrong number. He was either drunk, high, in jail, in the hospital, or dead. Or it was just a matter of coincidence that somebody dialed a wrong number from Arizona.

It wasn't a wrong number.

"Sam? Sam McElroy?" The woman's voice was low, deep, no doubt just coming off a hard cry or a binge.

"Yes, who is this, and why are you—"

"Sam who lived down the street from the Karlans long ago…" Her voice cracked, and she desperately tried to spit out the name without losing it altogether. "Holly Karlan?"

"Yes, that's me. Who is—"

"This is Holly's mother, Barbara. She was about to call you…" The crying erupted, and I tried to make out what Mrs. Karlan was saying. My number was displayed on Holly's phone, she was going to call me for some reason, never got around to it apparently.

"Is she all right, Holly…Holly all right?" I stuttered. I started to get up out of bed, moving to somehow hear better, make out Mrs. Karlan's words, keep Rachel at bay.

"Who is Holly?" asked Rachel over my shoulder. I ignored her, waved her away, but felt the dagger stare she was shooting at me.

"She's dead," said Barbara as clear as can be, the waterfall and the blubbering stopped cold. "Overdosed, is what they've told me. Not entirely unexpected, I suppose."

I hadn't spoken to Holly in a few years, but I had thought about her nearly every day since high school. The real Holly, the personable, the warm, the funny, the full-of-life-and-light Holly died long ago. Mrs. Karlan knew that, I was sure. Maybe it made this moment a little easier for her. Maybe not. We both knew it was inevitable. Still, it was hard to take, and the guilt sliced through me like a knife.

I thought briefly about the last time I saw her, just a glimpse of the real Holly, the person she was before. We kissed and did so much more than that, late one night, both drunk, in a small filthy apartment with no air conditioning. I didn't need much convincing to spend the night with her. For a little while, I felt like she had absolved me. For a little while, I felt free from the guilt. For a little while, I felt I could make Holly change back into the person she was before. Then she told me how much I needed to pay her for what we did, and that I needed to leave before Omar, her alcahuete, her chulo, she said, came home. "He doesn't like seeing the perdedores I bring home. But he likes seeing the dinero."

"Oh, I'm so sorry, Mrs. Karlan. I hadn't talked to her in a long time. I'm not sure why she would have tried to call me."

"Yeah, well, she may have been reaching out to someone, because they think she overdosed on purpose. A drug addict knows exactly how much is too much, they tell me, and this was, what term did the detective use? Oh yes, a 'massive overdose.' Not like the others that were on the fringe. This was over-the-top.

"Where do you live now? Are you still in Arizona? The funeral will be in a few days, I'm sure. I need to make arrangements. I'd like someone there who knew her back when...you know? Not those ingrates she hung around with as she got older. She had many men in her life. But I'd really like someone like you and that other boy who lived on the street there, if possible. Do you know who I am talking about?"

"I live in Illinois, near Chicago. But yes, I will come down. Yeah, sure, I'll come down for it," I stammered. "Yeah, Jimmer Cuddy still lives in Arizona. I'll call him. Again, I'm so sorry this happened, Mrs. Karlan."

I didn't know what else to say. I couldn't tell her I knew why her daughter was dead.

Her voice lowered to near a whisper. "She's with her father now, died of a heart attack, a broken heart I'm sure, just last year. I'll contact you soon with more infor- mation." And just like that, Mrs. Karlan's voice cut out.

"Who the fuck is Holly, and why do you look so glum?"

Who else, but Rachel. She was always this way. She didn't change, like Holly. When we met at Loyola, it was because she walked up to me and said, "Carry my back- pack to my next class." I did. She knew I had been steal- ing glances at her. When we got to the class, she said,

"How about we go to Crow's Nest tonight for a beer?" I said okay. She put my hand in her pants. Took my hands and cupped her breasts. Took my penis and put it in her when she was ready. Told me not to stop when I needed to stop and was agitated when it was suddenly over. I asked her to marry me because she told me to.

Rachel wore the pants, and I wore the skirt she picked out.

Short, chubby, and once cute. Rachel never whispered at all. She hollered, barked, commanded. Rachel was always a hard-ass, didn't laugh much, didn't even smile much. I was no better. I didn't laugh or smile much. I was never much to look at either. Medium height, medium build, brown hair, hazel but vacant eyes. Rachel once told me that I had vacant eyes. Not really a compliment. I told her she had pretty eyes, when I was really thinking she had cold, calculating, and manipulating eyes. She pointed out my receding hairline and my expanding waistline. I pointed out her receding waistline and expanding ingenuity.

When Elsa came along, Rachel seemed resentful, as if I had done something to disrupt her career, her precious independent lifestyle. Another person for her to manage. She hated being pregnant, and it took all I had to convince her how wonderful it was going to be. How we would cherish our little girl, and parenthood would bring us closer together as a couple. We did cherish our little girl, but it didn't bring us closer together as a couple.

When Elsa turned thirteen, she barely spoke to either one of us. She was embarrassed by her parents, her dull father and her pushy, irascible mother. She stayed over with friends every chance she could. When I asked her if she wanted to go to a Cubs game, she'd fold up her lips and grimace.

"Just us? I'd rather you drop me and my friends off and pick us up after it was over or something."

"You remind me so much of your mother," I'd reply.

So I told Rachel back then, after the phone call from Mrs. Karlan, as the sun was finally casting faint beams through the shades, about Holly, but I didn't tell her everything. I left out why Holly ended up the way she did, and I left out the brief time Holly and I spent together a few years back. I'm pretty sure she would have cut my balls off over both and left me, as it always appeared she wanted to do throughout our entire marriage. The only reason she never left was because I cooked, cleaned, and somewhat took care of Elsa. I was a houseboy. I didn't like being a houseboy, but I was content with it. Those duties and my boring-ass job writing articles about industrial safety solutions for trade publications kept me busy and kept my mind off the past.

***

"Rachel...Rachel...honey, turn over, please. You're dreaming...breathing...moaning right in my face. I can't sleep—"

"That was awesome, George."

"What? What was awesome? What are you dreaming about? Who's George?"

Rachel turned over. "Shhh, shut up, Sam, go back to sleep." She pulled the comforter up to her neck.

Two hours later, Sam was still lying there in the dark staring at the back of his wife.

She works with a George. Maybe she was just dreaming about work or something. Moaning? Are you a fuckin idiot? Oh, c'mon, it's not like you've never snapped out of a sex dream with a hard-

on before. Ever since that night with Holly a few years ago, if you can't fall right asleep, well, you just lie back and remember that and drift away peacefully, hoping desperately to have the ability to change the ending.

***

Sam stood gazing out the window.

Another police car. No lights flashing, it sat parked behind a gray Volkswagen that, by the smoke puffing from the exhaust pipe, looked to be still running. The cops, one stocky woman and one obese man, got out, adjusted their bulletproof vests accordingly, and lazily made their way to the Volkswagen, the male cop shaking his head, the female cop shrugging her shoulders.

"Doors are locked, I bet," said Sam to himself.

The two young men inside the Volks didn't move, not even when the large cop pounded on the driver's side window. Their heads were craned downward, bodies limp, sitting upright in the seats as if they just recently decided to take a little snooze on the way home from Chicago after a night of partying. Back to the burbs, where Mom would question where they'd been, and Dad wouldn't care one way or the other, already a lost cause. "Go throw your life away, son."

The belts hung loosely around their left arms. The hypodermic needles sat in their laps.

The young man sitting in the driver's seat finally jostled, turned his foggy eyes on the large cop.

"Unlock the door, now."

Too out of it to realize anything otherwise, the kid did as he was told.

"This is the second time in two years, Sam. You really want Elsa growing up in this neighborhood? For chrissake, half the people I work with live in Oak Park or River Forest. We should be living over there. We should be living out in Naperville or Barrington. If you didn't make such a shitty salary, maybe we wouldn't have drug addicts shooting up in front of our house."

"Hey, Rachel, that's not fair. Don't put this on me. I want to move to one of those towns just as much as you do. I'm not sure why you think I want to stay here. I have no love for Berwyn. If you recall, we both decided to buy this bungalow years ago—"

"I'm going to start looking," Rachel interrupted. "Enough is enough. This is bullshit."

"You wanted to send Elsa to private school, which I agree with, but we both know it would break the bank to try to sell now, recoup our losses, and try to find something that's reasonable in one of those towns. We're in the middle of a recession here. The real estate market has tanked."

"I'm going to start looking. You heard me. I don't need to be in an environment like this. I'm an executive, for chrissake. You know how embarrassing it is for me to tell people where I live?"

"When we bought this place we didn't have Elsa, and you loved it. You loved the proximity to the city, you loved the rows of bungalows, of two-flats, the racial mix, the blue-collar feel. We used to meet at that tavern on Roosevelt—"

"I don't give a shit. Times have changed. People change. I've changed. That old lady two blocks over got robbed last year, and there was that…whatever the hell it was when somebody was coming out of their garage, and somebody stabbed somebody…And those nasty gang wars in the city. You know what, stop wasting my time talking about this. I made up my mind. I'm going to look around. I don't give a damn if you want me to or not."

"I didn't say that—"

"Enough already! Don't you have to go out there and file a report, give a statement or something with those cops? Now go, get out of my face!"

Downtrodden, Sam turned from her and peered out the window. The two boys, their faces pale and blank, were standing handcuffed at the back of the Volks. The little female cop pulled items out of the car and placed them on the hood.

7

A Funeral

Cuddy nearly rolled his jeep making a turn, nearly smashed into a Lexus when the jeep's tires came screeching to a halt at a stoplight. He was panicked. He wished he had Valium, Librium, Xanax, or Ativan. Anything. He was sweating and shaking.

"Fuck! Why! Move! Move your fuckin cars!" He popped on his hazards and went over the curb, off-roading across a vacant lot.

When he reached the motel, he didn't even put the jeep in a parking space, just slammed on the brakes, jammed it to neutral, yanked up the emergency brake, and jumped out. He ran up the stairs and kicked in the door to room 22. The place was a mess, smelled of rotted garbage and mildew. Blankets, trash bags, dirty clothes, empty bottles. Stains on the stripped mattress.

Cuddy pictured her lying on the bed, drifting in and out of consciousness. He wondered if she had any regret as the end neared.

Did she feel anything? What was it like?

"I'm sorry, Holly." His back slid down the wall, and he sat down near the door. He tightened his face as best he could and tried to flex them away, but the tears streamed down, and he let out a deep sigh. He dug into the pocket of his sweatpants and pulled out his phone.

"How did you find out?"

"Her mother called me last night...I mean this morning," replied Sam. "Where are you? Why'd you hang up on me?"

"I'm at the motel where she had been staying, way down on Sixteenth and Baseline, a shithole called the Borgata, in fuckin Shitsville. I ran into her a few weeks ago outside a Laundromat. She looked like hell. Gave her a ride back here." There was a pause as Cuddy thought about what to say next. "She wanted drugs. Told her I didn't have those type of drugs." He paused again, looking at the bed, picturing her lying there. "This filthy fuckin place is where she died?"

"Yeah, overdosed. But her mom said cops think maybe suicide," answered Sam.

"It was suicide, even if she didn't mean to do it," said Cuddy starkly, staring at the bed. "She started killing herself way back when she was eighteen."

"I'm going to fly down for the funeral. Her mother wants us both there."

Cuddy wasn't listening to Sam anymore. "Someone is coming up the stairs. I'll call you back," he said.

"What?"

He only heard the footsteps, didn't see anyone yet. He had an idea of who it was, though. Holly's boyfriend. Some fuckin spic named Omar. He got up off the floor and braced himself with a solid stance, trying desperately not to jump too soon.

They stood face-to-face in the doorway, sizing each other up. Omar: younger, bald, ripped, tatted up, shiny gold front teeth, the rest crooked and stained. J. Cuddy: buzz-cut dirty-blond hair, ripped, tatted up, nice teeth. Omar: eyes of evil. J. Cuddy: eyes of rage.

"Where the fuck is Holly, muthafucka?"

The gears on Cuddy's chest fired up, and the rage struck first.

The throat.

His grip landed flush, and he backed Omar up against the outside railing. He heard the metal-on-metal clank, and it was as if Omar heard it too, and it reminded him of what he had.

A piece?

No.

Omar drew the six-inch blade from a sheath on his belt behind his back. It didn't faze Cuddy; only fed the rage. A blow to the face. Another blow to the face, trying to knock those goddamn gold teeth out of his mouth.

It's good to put your focus on something when you're lifting, a dot on the ceiling, a pretty girl's ass, the brain too preoccupied to register any pain.

With each punch: *Why-won't-those-teeth-come-out?!*

The knife sliced open Cuddy's left forearm, forcing him to release his grip of Omar's neck and halt the blows. Omar stooped and bullrushed. Cuddy was shoved back into the room.

Omar shouting, "I'm gonna gut you muthafucka!"

Cuddy landed atop a dresser, his broad shoulders sending a television crashing to the floor. Omar stayed on him, so Cuddy kicked at his body, pummeled his head with his fists, gouged at his eyes, and spit in his face, unaware exactly where the knife was or whose blood was splattering. A foot to the groin, a knee to the gut, a blow to the side of the head, back to the foot to the groin, this time a little higher and some leverage to shove this fucker off. It was his first real look at the knife as he flung Omar backward onto and over a small table by the window.

No time to waste. One more set, and then it's rest time. C'mon, Cuddy, this is when it's supposed to burn.

Before Omar could get both legs underneath him, he was quickly on the floor again, courtesy of a vicious blow that landed—

Bull's-eye!

—right smack on those gold teeth. It was as if Cuddy had thrown all of his 225-pound artificially chiseled frame into the punch. Omar's head had snapped back, and his body hit the floor. No more knife. His eyes remained open, but the evil had left them. They were wide, frightened, beginning to grow a frantic. He was breathing erratically, a rattle emanating from his chest, blood spitting from his mouth.

When Omar tried to say something, Cuddy could make out the dark gap where his front teeth had been, where those gold teeth used to be. Omar clutched his chest and began to breathe harder. At first Cuddy thought maybe he was dying.

Heart attack? Torn artery or something?

The teeth were in Omar's lungs. Cuddy grunted a laugh but then squinted and peered inquisitively at the shit bag while picking up the knife.

"Huh, yer gonna wanna get those nuggets out of there, muchacho." He tossed the blade onto Omar's chest and walked out.

Relief. Maybe a hike up Camelback, take the Chollo Canyon trail this time. Maybe knock out a few dead lifts at the gym. Maybe stop by the prick's mansion and break his teeth in.

Bounding down the stairs, he looked at the gash across his right forearm, a lightning bolt of blood streaking through the motorcycle chick with the big tits and the jet-black hair.

Holly Karlan.

***

Cuddy and I didn't speak much on the drive from the airport to the cemetery in Avondale. The warm air blowing through the open jeep made it difficult anyway. There really wasn't much to say. We both knew this day would come eventually. It was inevitable. Holly was on a path of self-destruction, and nothing, not even my night with her a few years back, when I laid it all out for her and briefly thought I had made a connection again, was going to change anything.

We were both dressed in suits, sweating from the heat. Cuddy had a pissed off look on his face, his jaw clenched. I noticed the bandage on his forearm but didn't inquire. The bruised knuckles I noticed later, when they were lowering the urn into the ground. He had only nodded when I got into the jeep at the airport. He had quickly turned up the music, blasted out of there, through the valley, beyond the mountains and down along flat stretches of nothing land. Out where there's no life, alongside a water canal. Perfect place to go be dead, I suppose.

"They were fine with the cremation," was the first thing Mrs. Karlan said to us. "Well, I guess the Catholic Church really has changed its ways. But it was her wish, so I honored it. Even her…she deserves to be sent off the way she wanted to be…" She started to cry.

I put my hand on her shoulder, tried my best to console the poor mother who only wanted the very best for her daughter, her only child. I wanted to tell her she raised her well. It was just circumstances that led to this. Fucked-up circumstances that J. Cuddy and I had a hand in.

"They asked if I wanted to keep the ashes, but I really don't have any use for…" she choked up again. "So…the burial." When she raised her head she looked a lot older, full of wrinkles and blue hair. She'd gone through so much with her daughter, and it seemed to have drained the life from her.

I looked around the parking lot to see who else would be at this ceremony, but there was no one. The three of us stood in the middle of this treeless place, melting in the heat as four pounds of Holly Lynn Karlan's ashes were lowered into the ground, the urn a hand-crafted box made of cedar with little hearts and doves carved into the side.

I couldn't hold back the tears, and soon they ran down from under my sunglasses. Looking at those hearts, I pictured two Hollys: The little girl who lived down the street, always willing and wanting to play with Cuddy and me, always letting us rescue her from imaginary sinking ships or burning buildings, pirates, robbers, always letting us catch her when she'd bounce off the trampoline in her backyard. The Holly whom I walked home from school with almost every day, talking about the future. The Holly who kissed me at the eighth-grade dance, just before we were going into the gym. She took my hand, stepped behind me, and let me lead her in, as if I were unafraid, not at all the shy one.

And the other Holly, the one I spent the night with just a few years ago, the one who made me feel alive again. The one who smiled at me as if I were her savior, her superhero, her knight. I'll never forget what she said, what she whispered into my ear while we were clutched in each other's arms. "I've missed you, Sam McElroy."

Standing there in the heat, I just kept hearing those words whispered in my ear over and over again. "I've missed you, Sam McElroy." It was as if maybe I was saying them to myself.

Afterward we both gave Mrs. Karlan a hug and briefly talked about what we were both doing now. When I told her I had a daughter, she only shook her head and said, "Well, good luck." Cuddy didn't say much, not even when Mrs. Karlan reminded us of the time Holly fell off her bike and scraped her knee up, and Cuddy carried her home while I pushed the bike back. Mrs. Karlan said it was that image that made her want to call me and ask that we be there for the funeral.

I wasn't surprised Cuddy didn't shed a tear. But he looked like he wanted to annihilate something. His face was red, the shades covered his eyes, but I know they were probably stone cold.

"Let's go drink some beers," he said, climbing into the jeep.

At the bar, he took a swig, popped the bottle down, and turned to me. "I've been watching him."

"Who?"

Annoyed, he said again, "Him."

"Why?"

"For a while now, every so often, I drive up there, park the jeep on a side road, and hike to his place. I just sit between the rocks and the cacti and watch. Sometimes I follow him and his boys around.

"He's fuckin rich, lives up beyond Carefree near the Tonto Forest in a mansion the size of a warehouse on the side of a fuckin mountain." Another swig. "And he's still a fuckin douche bag."

"What do you mean?"

"You remember Sherry Pendleton from school, younger than us?"

"Sort of."

"Well, she's a trainer at one of the gyms I frequent that I fuck once in a while, and one night she was telling me about her friend who went home with this older guy after clubbing, former local pro ballplayer, lives on the side of a mountain in a mansion. She told Sherry that all kinds of crazy shit must have went on. But she couldn't recall everything."

"Who, Sherry?"

What little patience Cuddy had was waning. "No, the friend couldn't recall everything. When she woke up the next day, she was hurtin and pierced and had lashes across her back and shit. Sherry thinks her friend got slipped something in her drink. Told her to go to the cops, but the friend would have none of that. Said he was real sweet, gave her a bunch of stuff, and hopes maybe she'll hook up with him again sometime."

"Jesus, why didn't she go to the cops?"

He threw me a stern look. He didn't have to say it. I knew what he was thinking by the hardness in his eyes, which said, "Why didn't we ever go to the cops, asshole," without his actually saying it.

I drew back, surprised, swigged my beer, looked at my long-lost best friend curiously. "What are you doing stalking him?"

He turned away from me, peered into the mirror behind the bar, said, "Because, I want to kill him."

We drank more. Talked about nothing. I wanted Rory dead just as much as Cuddy. I wanted him to pay. Long ago Cuddy and I discussed burying him somewhere in a canyon, maybe up near Monumental Valley or somewhere in the Chuska Mountains. Who would find him? But we always wrestled with how and why. And wasn't it really just all talk? I mean, this was the real world. Not a video game or a movie. We should have gone to the cops that night when we were eighteen. We should have beat the shit out of him that night, like Cuddy wanted to do. We should have done this, and we should have done that. I wondered then if Cuddy was serious.

Did he really want to find a way this time?

We went back to his townhouse and changed clothes. He said he wanted to take me on a hike up Camelback Mountain, to something called the Praying Monk.

"Why?" I asked.

"Because it's where I go to think."

8

Chains

She feels it, but can't determine the sensation itself, the stress of her muscles, the tension on her body. She sees him but doesn't recognize who or what he is. Her vision is murky; a thin, opaque film lies over her pupils. Her hearing is shrouded by a denseness, the sound waves deep and stretched out. She can't feel scared. She can't feel afraid. She can't feel nervous. She can't feel happy. She can't feel sad. She can't feel angry. She can't feel anything but a veiled desire, a gentle euphoria.

It doesn't matter anymore how she got this way. It doesn't matter what's happening. The chemicals have entered the bloodstream and altered the brain. Reason is temporarily dormant. All of her choices she considers righteous.

She is facing down, looking through flashes of strobe lights. There is loud electronic dance-club music playing. There is a leather bridle around her head attached to a red gag ball wedged in her mouth. Her arms are stretched back behind her, her legs are bent upward and back at the knees, and there are shackles on her wrists and ankles. There is a large thick chain attached to the shackles. There is another large thick chain attached to that chain that leads up to an industrial-size slip hook embedded into a beam in the ceiling.

She is naked. Her wrists are shackled behind her to her ankles and she is suspended in the air a foot or so over a bed, over a man wearing nothing but a leather mask. He has pinched holes into her nipples, and licked the blood through the slot of his mask. He has attached pins to the nipples. The man has run a smaller chain through the pins and attached it to a leather strap around her neck.

He has rigged it so that if she raises her head, the chain attached to the pins in her nipples will tighten. He has rigged it so that when she lowers her head, the leather strap around her neck will cinch and begin to strangle her.

He tautly wraps a leather strap around his own neck and begins to watch her.

Every time she moves her head up or down, he tightens the leather strap around his neck.

He is getting off on his own asphyxiation, on the torture he is inflicting on her and himself, on her incapacity to do anything about any of it.

He has now unhooked the leather band that goes from the chain to her breasts. He has taken off the bridle around her head and the leather strap around her neck. He has taken out the red gag ball in her mouth. He is tightening the leather band around his own neck again with one hand and slashing her back with a riding crop with the other.

After a while, the strobe lights, the electronic dance-club music turn off, the lights of the bedroom turn on, and the man sits Indian-style in front of her head on the bed.

He places his two fingers under her chin and pulls her head up to look him in the eyes. She is moaning incoherently, saliva dripping from her mouth. Due to the chemicals in her bloodstream, she has a slight grin on her face.

Her eyes meet his but don't register anything out of the ordinary, though the moaning becomes more pronounced. He nods and accepts that, through the chemically induced drug haze, she is enjoying the torture.

9

Faithful Friends

Y ou look like you've muscled up more from the last time I saw you," said Sam, following Cuddy on a trail that leads up Camelback Mountain.

"Yeah?" Cuddy, in a black muscle shirt and camouflage cargo shorts, backpack full of climbing ropes and harnesses, glanced at his biceps and looked down at his pecs. *Those are the best compliments.*

"You still...on that stuff?"

"What the fuck you care?"

"I don't know, man. That stuff can probably cause major problems in the long run."

"Yeah, well, we're all gonna die of somethin sometime. At least I'm enjoyin my life." *Well, I am when I'm not arguing with myself. When I'm not having bouts with depression. When I'm not acting hysterical.* "Not like you."

They began to climb the actual rock steps sunk into the ground, the slope getting rockier, less populated by the shrubs and the blackbrush trees.

"What do you mean by that?"

"You seem like you live in misery, Sammy," replied Cuddy over his shoulder. "Like every day is dark and ominous. Your dream always to be a cynical prick?"

"Is your dream to have the biggest body and the smallest dick in the world?"

They both laughed. This eased the mood, friends razzing each other for their personal faults, just like old times, but knowing, deep down, they cared greatly for one another. As they hiked farther up toward the forehead of the camel-shaped mountain, and the heat rose from the valley floor, Sam groaned. "Why are you making me do this?"

"It's good for you, Sammy Mac. Yer gettin a bit soft."

Cuddy spat out instructions as they made their way farther up the mountain. He'd been hiking and climbing Camelback for years. Not everything made sense up on the mountain overlooking the valley, but things became clearer. He looked over at the rock tower called the Praying Monk.

Decisions in life aren't based on fear up there. There is no fear up there. It's just you and the land and the people out before you. The streetlights delineating the routes here and there. You're free to take different paths, Cuddy.

He continued to climb in silence.

Look at the decisions you've made to get you where you are, some poor decisions, some not so poor. You've made your own way.

Nobody helped you, except for Coach. This is where you'll decide to take a step into the great unknown.

"This is called the Flaming Testicle," he finally said aloud to Sam without turning around. They stood perched on a narrow cliff near an imposing boulder. Cuddy retrieved the ropes and the harnesses from his backpack and prepped Sam for the climb. "Just stay a few feet behind. When we get to the headwall, I'll go up and across and belay you."

"Belay me, what the fuck does that mean?"

"Rope, me, up there holding it. You climbing up."

"Really?"

"Don't be worried. This is the shit I'm talking about with you. You need to get out there on the ledge and start living. Otherwise, you're just waiting around to die." He turned and faced the headwall and started his climb.

When they reached the forehead of the camel, they hiked over to the base of the Praying Monk, an eighty-foot-high red sandstone rock formation. Sam was surprised by its massiveness. It wasn't so imposing when looking up at it from the valley. He looked at the bandage on Cuddy's forearm and decided to finally inquire.

"A brawl at a bar?" He pointed at the wound.

"Holly's boyfriend, Omar. Punched the teeth out of his mouth with one blow at that seedy motel she was living at in the slums of South Phoenix, the Borgata." He grunted.

"No shit?"

"Fucker came up the stairs and asked where she was, didn't even know…" His voice trailed off.

Sam remembered Holly mentioning Omar when he spent the night with her a few years back. He wondered if Cuddy knew the guy was a member of a Phoenix gang and more her pimp than a boyfriend. He decided to change the subject. Looking around at the view, he said, "This is nice. This is where you go to think?"

Cuddy only looked at him bemused and began to ascend the southeast corner of the tower, threading the rope line through premade bolts in the sandstone. "I'll help you up once I get there."

"We're going to the top of it?"

"Nothing gets past you, Sammy Mac."

The sandstone itself wasn't hot, but the cobbles along the route were turning warm in the sun. Cuddy made his way up the tower rather quickly and belayed Sam, who took his time, peering up every so often for an assuring look.

Look at him up there, a badass, kickin the shit out of gang-bangers, scoring hot young women while in his early forties, and scaling mountains just to go think. Doing whatever the hell he wants in life. Maybe that night, or the military shit, changed him for the good. I mean, he's a hothead, but at least he doesn't doubt what he's sure of.

"It's awesome up here, isn't it." It wasn't a question, more a confirmation. Looking out over the valley to the horizon, to Squaw Peak and Mummy Mountain, Cuddy sighed and nodded to himself. He could tell by the look on his friend's face that the view was magnificent. They found a spot to sit, and Cuddy reached into the backpack and pulled out two cans of beer.

"They ain't cold, but what the hell."

They raised the cans, and Sam said the toast in a quiet and dismal tone. "To Holly. She's free."

After a few minutes, Cuddy looked at Sam knowingly. He was going to say something serious. "You ever pray for anything?"

"No, not really."

"You believe in God, heaven, something?"

"I believe in heaven."

"Yeah, well yer an idiot."

"What, Cuddy, you don't believe in anything?"

"No, I believe in something. I believe this is all an illusion. That what's happening here and everywhere isn't really happening at all. We're just stuck here...for now."

"You climb up here and sit on this thing called the Praying Monk and ponder such things?"

Cuddy turned toward Sam, squinting. "I've thought real hard about some stuff over the years. Maybe it's time. I could use my hunting rifle...my Remington, pick him off from maybe three hundred, four hundred yards away. No one would know what or why. Let the cops scratch their heads over it, and then it gets thrown into a cold case file."

"Could you do it?"

"Shoot from that far out? Sure. I told you about the bighorn sheep I took down with Coach a few years ago."

"No, shoot him? Kill him?"

A warm breeze blew up from the valley. Sam welcomed any air he could get. His body was far removed from being acclimated to the Arizona heat.

Cuddy looked away, gazing off toward another mountain in the far distance. "Yeah, I wouldn't have any problem with that. Before I got booted from the military, I fucked some people up pretty good. A few Iraqi soldiers ran from a burning tank in Al Khafji. We opened up on them with M4s before the Air Force opened up on us."

"It'd have to be someplace without video cameras, and that seems unheard of nowadays."

"He and his guys take dirt bikes out on trails through the foothills up by where he lives. There's nothing out there but junipers and cacti. They go out there shooting guns, too. So maybe it could look like an accident."

"Your rifle, you bought it legitimately, went through a background check? Even with"—he paused—"what happened in the military?"

"Yeah, it's easy to buy guns in Arizona. It's the most gun-friendly state in America. You can walk around with a gun in a holster if you want to. You can go into Pete's Gun Shop and walk out with a fuckin Uzi."

"They can match bullets to guns," said Sam. "Maybe they could match the bullet they found in his head to your rifle. And what if you missed, and they came after you, the cops or him and his guys?"

"We've been talking about doing something like this to this asshole for years, and you're still worried about the consequences?" Cuddy swigged his beer and looked out at the horizon, a sunset in its infancy.

"There have to be no consequences, no risk. That's the point, or it's all for nothing. What if someone happened to see you or made out your jeep in the area? Connections are easy to come by these days with cell phone pings, satellites, GPS, and whatnot. Hell, Cuddy, the second you search something on the Internet, Google or someone is creating a dossier of you and your interests, maybe even your thoughts."

Discontented, Cuddy sighed. His head was filling with conflicting emotions. He didn't want to tell Sam he was having sporadic episodes of not caring anymore. He didn't want to tell him that maybe someday he'd drive his jeep right up that stone driveway, through the portico and into the front door, and just start shooting whoever he saw in that big house. He'd eventually get around to Rory James.

He did not want to tell him about the severe depression that had been consuming him, the wicked thoughts, the verbal quarrels he'd been having with himself. He didn't want to tell Sam he worried about his mind-set, that maybe he was headed down the same path as his father or Holly. He hadn't been himself lately, nightmares and flashbacks from that disaster in Al Khafji decades ago. The images of his father lying on the floor, head in a pool of blood, of Holly in that bed long ago, comatose.

He was losing interest in everything—even gave a stern warning to an Arizona State University baseball player about the effects of PEDs. "Are you gonna sell me the stuff or not?" the kid had asked. Coach went ballistic on that one, threatened to cut him loose if he didn't get his act together.

"What if…" Sam had a thought, but it needed work. "If we somehow got the girl that this Sherry is friends with to go to the cops…" He knew he was pulling at straws. "Maybe if we told her about what happened to Holly years ago, maybe she'd want to do something."

"Do you want him living and breathing, or do you want him dead?" Cuddy crushed the can with one hand and shoved it into the backpack. "He's got boo-koo money now, Sam. He'd hire a few high-priced lawyers and get off on a technicality. Besides, he destroyed her life. He should have his life destroyed."

"But do you really think that what happened set her on such a shitty course that it caused her to make such horrible decisions…I mean, if she had gotten help afterward, maybe she'd be a mom living in the valley, working as a teacher or an executive at a big company and playing tennis at the club or something, living a good life. Maybe she would have made better decisions, decisions that would have forced her to take the right path."

"Maybe she would have married you?"

Sam's eyebrows rose. "Yeah, maybe."

"When you're eighteen, Sam, you're vulnerable. Hell, doesn't matter how old you are, your experiences in life influence who you are. Look what it's done to us, we're still talking about it some twenty-five years later. I'm not gonna blame her for not trying to get her life on track afterward. That's tough to do when you've had something horrible done to you."

Cuddy stood up and looked down. "But you're right, we can try to fly, or we can continue to fall."

Spiral is a better word.

He nodded while looking down the steep slope.

"Let's forget all this, get on with our lives. You stop being miserable, and I'll stop being…," he turned and looked at Sam, "me."

He reached out his hand.

Sam took it, and Cuddy stood him up. They shook hands. Bro-hugged.

"All right, sounds like the best plan," said Sam.

A smile spread across Cuddy's face, the first Sam had seen in years. But it hinted danger.

"Now, let's have some fun and repel down!"

10

Caborca

Caborca again," Cortez sighed to himself, "twice in the last month I been ordered to monitor the shipments. Greedy border patrol with its spot inspecciónes, muy dinero, muy dinero. Chrise, the bastards makin more than me. Perhaps I should get a job on the border."

He turned the Escalade down a forlorn street with dilapidated buildings and open-air metal sheds. "Fuckin town, dust and palm trees."

Looking in the rearview mirror, he watched as Hosk made the turn in the twelve-foot-long unmarked moving truck. The truck went up onto a curb and nearly hit a light post before straightening back out onto the road.

"Hosk, you drawing too much atención!" Cortez said aloud to himself. "Is this what happens every time we make a run?"

In front of a gate leading up to a driveway, he brought the Escalade to a stop. A large Mexican man with an automatic weapon slung over his shoulder waddled to the truck. In Spanish he told Cortez to get out. A quick frisk. He peered into the back of the Escalade. Nothing. "Usted puede entrar," said the man. The gate opened.

As he drove through the entrance, Cortez watched in the mirror as the guard frisked Hosk and checked the truck. He saw him lumber up into the back. *No doubt*, thought Cortez, *looking in the empty coolers*.

At the end of the driveway, Cortez pulled up to a white but weathered adobe with iron grates on the windows. A short stocky man with thin gray hair, wearing jeans, white shirt, and suede vest, and with a chrome-plated handgun stuffed into his waist, walked out of the house and stood in the driveway.

"Mejor amigo!" he shouted at Cortez.

A few feet behind the stocky man, a big Mexican man with slicked-back black hair, a thick black mustache, and dressed in black down to his cowboy boots emerged in the door frame. He stood behind the short stocky man with his arms crossed in front of him. Cortez recognized him—Renato Velasquez, muscle from the core of the cartel. Which cartel, he wasn't sure. The Zetas, the Sinoloas, the Gulf cartel? Didn't matter. He wasn't supposed to know and didn't want to know. Knowing could get you killed, get your head chopped clean off. Renato's presence ensured one thing: Cortez and Hosk would again get a personal escort back across the American side of the border. That put him at ease but just a little. Renato was unpleasant to work with, much like his boss, Rory James, but scary in a different way.

"Then what the fuck you carrying that gun for, viejo sabio?" said Cortez.

The old man looked at the gun. "Ah, protección." He gestured toward Renato Velasquez. "We shoot you in thee face, you try to steal from us."

"When have we never paid, wise old man?" Cortez got out of the Escalade, shaking his head.

Hosk pulled the truck up to another closed gate next to the house, this one with a driveway leading back behind the home.

"We've had some unfortunate incidents down here recently. You—you and your employer—very good with paying. But one cannot be too careful."

"What do you mean incidents?" asked Cortez. "All the times I've driven down here, I've never been stopped at that gate. Heck, that gate has never been closed."

"Ah, da times have changed, amigo." He gestured toward Renato again. "Thee powers that be want to keep a close eye on things now, even us so-called little players. Trust hard to come by."

"Yeah, well, things changing for us, too, old man. Same mercancías, but we reducing the amount of everything, the H, the coke, the somatropin, the zacate, the crank, everything."

The old man began to frown. "Well, ah corz. China ain't doing us any favors, amigo, thee wholesale price of pharmaceutical ingredients is skyrocketing. Thee US government cracking down on the synthetic testosterone and everything associated with it. Shit, even Tamoxifen." Now the old man grinned coyly. "Sí, thee times have changed." A grunt, boisterous and phlegmy. "It ain't thee seventies with cocaine, amigo. It ain't thee eighties with crack. It ain't thee nineties with heroin. It ain't ten years ago with meth. Weed, fer fuck's sake, legal in some states in that country!" He looked up at the sky, sighed, and then began to drift off into thought while still speaking.

"All them boats jammed to the top of thee hulls with marijuana at thee bottom of the Pacific off the Baja shore. All them little jumper planes that went down in thee Sonora desert stocked full of thee stuff. All them miles of underground tunnels. All them people shot up.

"Now, amigo, I hear you can go into a little store in Colorado and buy thee stuff right off the rack. Hell, thee opium fields are drying up here! El Chapo is rotting in a jail! How's a Mexican cartel supposed to make a livin if not by being innovative?"

"Well, it ain't all bad news, old man. My boss says he'd like to start pushing the mix he had you and your crew working on, the…" Cortez cleared his throat, "the roofie-like product you been given him samples of. Wants more of it to sell and less of the other stuff."

The old man's silver eyebrows went up.

"He ready to expand it," said Cortez.

"He like thee last sample batch, huh?" said the old man, nodding.

"Sí," answered Cortez, "very much."

"Yer boss, who been makin all them deals over thee years for thee muscle products we get from thee nips, and these"—the old man gestured toward the moving truck—"these pequeño shipments of heroin, coke, weed, meth is ready to go in a different direction?"

Cortez blinked and swallowed. He'd never seen the old man so agitated before. Renato Velasquez looked just as perturbed. "Sí," he muttered. "Sounds to me like you may have already been manufacturing—"

"Ah corz, we business people down here, amigo. And business people must make a livin. It's gonna cost you." The old man nodded.

Cortez knew better than to get into a pissing match with these people. Sure, Rory James helped concoct the drug and would be livid when he heard the old man was manufacturing it and selling it to others, but he'd spin that somehow when he got back to the mansion, or maybe not mention that little fact at all. You didn't argue with these people. You placated them.

"Well, I'm tired of making these eleven-hour round-trip drives anyway. It's time we just trust one another and get back to our regular shipments. Back to the one-stop shopping we've come to depend on from you." Cortez nervously wiped his brow and tried to smile. It was getting hotter in this hellhole.

"I sell you veinte diez-galone buckets of thee powder."

Cortez looked surprised. "You have that, ten-gallon buckets of it? Jesus. That's enough ta…"

Start a drug empire.

"We mass producing, amigo. Thee formula yer boss kindly give us is taking off, just thee right blend of rivotril, GHB, and cantharidin. Thee drug of thee future. You probably won't be buying from me directly this time next year. I'll be mayorista, a megawholesaler, un comerciante grande rica en grasas. I'll be on a beach somewhere in thee Bahamas."

Cortez tried to look into the adobe, through the bars, through the house itself to the backyard, where there was a large steel shed. He'd never been allowed back there before. "You producing everything here, old man?" he asked more than just curiously.

"Sí, hence all the armas."

"How many people you got back there workin for you?"

"Ah, now you ask too many questions, amigo. Best get drogas and be on your way. You get it up there, spread it 'round, sell it high. Entiendes?"

Cortez looked around. "I get twenty ten-gallon buckets in the truck, plus three hundred kilos of H and coke, plus thee pharms, thee meth, plus a couple crates of M27s safely across the border?"

"We take you to thee border, make sure you get through. Like before." The old man gestured once again toward the big Mexican in black, Renato Velasquez. "Mi amigo know his way 'round thee desert and thee border. You should trust him by now."

Cortez let the laughing subside. He knew Velasquez was there to escort him safely out of Mexico, but he wanted to make sure, and he wanted the old man to say it in front of Velasquez. He didn't want the big man in black getting any harebrained ideas that he was an easy mark, though he certainly was.

"Good thing I bring all this dinero with me," Cortez said as he began to walk back behind the Escalade. He opened the rear gate and lifted up a compartment. The old man took the silver handled pistol from his waistband. Velasquez reached around his back and pulled out some sort of Uzi handgun. He darted a look at Hosk, who was still sitting motionless in the cab of the truck. The men walked over to the Escalade, their eyes on Cortez.

Cortez unzipped two duffel bags full of cash and grinned proudly.

The old man peered into the back of the vehicle, scratching his chin. "Yer gonna need a lot more dinero, amigo," he said dryly.

11

Pistols

I was drunk and high, and Cuddy dragged me to a seedy strip club in old Phoenix. I had flown in two days earlier, and we had gotten together with a few other old high school buddies and seen a football game at Sun Devil Stadium. Rachel let me go because she had been in San Francisco for work an entire week, and I had been busy with Elsa and my own job. Oh, and I had begged.

This was my last night. I was flying back to Chicago the next morning. Some of the guys had started out with us on this night but had opted out hours ago. I was ready to call it a night, but Cuddy was adamant we stop here first. It was sometime after midnight.

There were fat Mexicans drinking tequila and Tecates at small tables, a deep bass pumping through large speakers on each wall. We sat near one of the walls, ordered two Coronas. Three women went up onto a small stage one by one, and the crowd seemed disappointed. Each one was introduced: Destiny, Cinnamon, Eve. One showing it all too early, one with too many rolls, one with no rhythm, no style.

But then...She was skinnier than the other dancers, tatted up—one arm entirely covered in ink, rose garland wrapping around the entire limb like a hunter-green snake. She wore more makeup than clothes. She was wearing black high-heeled shoes, jean shorts, and a black halter top. Her black hair—so black it was raven—obviously dyed, was pulled back into a ponytail. When she hit the stage, she looked innocent—even with the tats, even with the ample breasts, the long silky legs, the full lips, the sharp blue eyes—innocent, but also experienced and wise to the scene. She was older than all the others, but that also seemed to be an asset. She was a woman, knew her way around the stage and the pole. I didn't recognize her at first, the name didn't register, too focused on her curves, her moves, her exotic look, her grace.

"Wow, she's unbelievable. There's something intoxicating about her," I said to Cuddy.

He took a swig and smiled. "Yeah, I thought you'd think so." I just figured he had seen this particular dancer before.

She stripped off her jean shorts first, not by letting them just drop to the floor, but slowly and provocatively shimmying out of them, revealing black silk French-cut panties—not a thong like most of the girls. Just her up there, with long black hair, in black halter top, black panties, inked up, she moved poetically. Smiled effortlessly.

At that moment, I didn't sense a sadness behind the smile.

God, Rachel would kill me if she knew I was here.

The thought of my wife screaming at me faded into obscurity when she turned her back on us, crossed her arms, reached for the bottom of her halter top, and began to raise it up over her head. Each inch revealing more skin, more ink, all sorts of designs: more roses, skulls, headstones, barbed wire, daggers. The Mexicans went wild, whistling, shouting their broken English. Cash began to litter the stage.

The pistols looked holstered into the back of the panties. We could only see the handles. They were there etched on each side of her lower waist. She bent over and took the panties off.

When she finally stood back up, we could see the long barreled pistols were pointed at an angle down toward her ass. In between the guns was a cross with the words "Only the Strong Survive."

When she turned around, the ponytail was gone and that long raven hair streamed down over her shoulders. There were more tats around her breasts, across her flat stomach—little birds, stars, hearts, and a bright monarch butterfly on her lower abdomen. A ring in her bellybutton.

She waved at the howls, picked up her clothes and her money, and when the DJ said her name again, it finally hit me.

"Let's give a big hand for Holly Hellraiser! For those of you who want to get a better look at those tattoos, she's available for lap dances, private or group!"

I turned to Cuddy, an expression of surprise and anger battling it out in my face. He only nodded. I felt ashamed. I felt pissed off. I didn't want to look at the strippers anymore. I didn't want to drink anymore. I didn't want to be there anymore. I wasn't comfortably drunk and high anymore.

"Why'd we come here, asshole?"

"That's it, Sammy Mac, you're finally showing some life."

He could tell I wasn't amused. He shrugged those massive shoulders. "I just figured that maybe you'd want to see her."

I could tell he felt a little ashamed. I could tell it made him a little uncomfortable, too.

He put the beer bottle on the table and leaned over. "Look, I ran into her here a few weeks ago and...I don't know...maybe I just wanted you to see her, too...maybe you could talk to her. She looks good, but she's doing this, and she's still a fuckin junkie. I've tried to talk to her. Nothin." He leaned back again in his chair. "But she asks 'bout you every time I see her, man."

I watched her work the room, back to being clothed, but letting all those bloodshot eyes molest her cleavage while she bent over to whisper in their faces. The music, the howling, it was muted in my head. I could see Holly Karlan in there, under the makeup, the tattoos. I could see her and me holding hands, running for the school bus down a dusty sidewalk, our whole lives out before us. What would we become?

She saw Cuddy first—all the women did. Her eyes lit up, and she rushed over. He stood and put his arms around her. I was nervous, not knowing whether to stand or remain seated, to be thrilled to see her like this or embarrassed to see her like this. Hesitantly, I stood.

That moment between songs, between whistles, between shouts, between bottles clinking. "Hi, Holly." I said it without any emotion whatsoever, a hoarse spit of three syllables.

She turned. Her mouth fell open. I could see the silver glint of a barbell tongue ring.

"Oh shit, Sam," she said. That tattooed arm went up, her hand to her mouth as if to close it or cover it. On cue, the bass thumping. A petite redhead took the stage. Holly was around the table and around me in one swift motion, those thin, inked-up arms wrapping my neck, those ample breasts pressing into my chest, that long raven hair to my face and lips. I held her tight, breathed her in, wanted to pick her up and get her the fuck out of that shithole, take her someplace nice.

When we finally released, she looked up at me, cupping my face in her hands, smiling wildly, her eyes tearing up. I could see the lines in her face even through the heavy makeup. I could see the freshly whitened teeth, probably covering up the rot. I could see the years of heartache, of struggle. I could see the hardship, the suffering, the many desperate personas. But through it all, I could still see Holly, that girl who lived down the block, the girl I grew up with, racing our bikes down the street, laughing in the summer heat, swimming in the pools, chasing each other at the birthday parties, the block parties. Holly, the girl holding my hand before we went into that grade-school dance. Holly, the first girl I ever kissed. Holly, the girl on my lap in the packed car zipping down the two-lane on its way out to the desert party. Holly Karlan.

It wouldn't be until dawn when I'd again see the girl I had let down.

A big guy came over, his eyes burning a hole into Holly. "Customer," she said to him. "Private show." I peered at Cuddy, but he was preoccupied with about three strippers all wanting his attention…and maybe his money. Holly took my hand and directed me back to a small room with a couch. She reached behind me and closed a curtain. I sat and she perched herself on the arm of the couch.

Her tattooed hand went to my shoulder. "How you been?"

"Good," I lied. *I've been miserable, as always. Just ask Cuddy. Been that way most of my life.*

She looked at my ring. "Who's the lucky girl?"

"Oh, yeah, I'm married—Rachel. We have a daughter, Elsa."

"That's great, Sam."

"How about you?" The question was odd, being holed up in a private room of a strip club and all.

"Ah, I still don't know what love means."

A sobering silence. I felt the same way.

"You know what," she said, standing up. "I'm due a sick day. Let's get out of here. Go get some drinks and catch up."

"That sounds great. Let's do that, Holly." When I stood up she just gazed at me. I wanted to hold her in my arms again, too.

Cuddy, the redhead, Holly, and I went to a bar and got drunk on beer and liquor and stories of when we were young. Afterward, Cuddy and the redhead disappeared, staggering arm in arm into the darkness, while Holly and I jumped into a cab. We were going to her place. She didn't want me out of her sight.

I got the impression she didn't want to be alone.

12

Blue Steel

Elsa had left for school, and Rachel for the train station. No one had said goodbye to anyone, except for me. Standing on the front porch, I hollered out, "Have a nice day, ladies," as they went off in opposite directions, Elsa with her headphones on, Rachel looking at work e-mails on her phone. I sensed both of them rolling their eyes. Rachel yelled back without turning around, "Windows!"

I had taken the day off to clean all the windows in the house. Rachel's idea. "Okay," I replied. "I can do that."

It was in a long dark-blue sock under a hydrangea in front of the porch. I only saw the end of the sock first. I reached for it and pulled it out from under leaves and sticks. I figured some kids in the neighborhood had dropped it or something. Maybe the wind had blown it into our yard. I was just going to throw it away then get down to the business of washing those windows.

But it was heavy, and it sagged as I held it while walking back up the steps toward the front door. I was fumbling with it as I walked back inside, a little concerned about what was in it. It was hard and oddly shaped. I rolled back the sock and saw a black grip. I sat down on the couch. Rolled back a little more. It was a gun. A toy gun? No bright-red plastic plug at the end. A revolver of some sort. A prop gun, I assumed.

But then I saw what looked to be real bullets in the chamber, the gold caps. I quickly put it down next to me and got up. I rushed over to my cell phone on the kitchen table and began to call 911 but stopped. You don't call 911 for something like this. It's not an emergency. That gun sitting on my couch in my living room isn't going to rise up and shoot me. I thought about calling Rachel; she'd tell me what to do with it. (Probably tell me to put it to my head and pull the trigger.) There's a nonemergency number, or I could call Dale. He'd know what to do with it. Probably come get it.

Dale Bonner was a Berwyn cop who lived down the street, nice guy, nice young family. Dale and I had been out mowing our lawns one Saturday afternoon when we got to talking about all the crime recently in the area. He told me Berwyn was a nice location for the suburban kids to stop at and shoot up the heroin they purchased on the West Side of Chicago before heading home. "It's completely random, the neighborhoods they choose," he had said. "The holdups we occasionally get are usually connected to gang initiation. They pop over here, scare the shit out of someone, maybe steal some cash or a smartphone. That way they're not sticking a gun in the face of someone from their own turf or someone in a rival gang who might shoot back."

Dale said Chicago had gotten worse than LA and New York in regards to gang murders; called it "the new murder capital of America."

It made sense. Live next to a big city with that moniker attached to it, you're going to have crime spilling over every once in a while.

I stood there staring at the gun. Moved a few steps closer to it. It wasn't exactly on par with today's handguns seen on television or in video games, those crazy semiautomatic pistols with clips that held ten or more rounds. This looked old-fashioned compared to those. Long barrel, maybe four inches. Blue steel. Rubber grip. Six shots. Every number and letter on the gun looked to be filed off.

I went to the laptop and toggled through some images. Found one that looked similar. A Smith & Wesson .38 Special with double action—I had to look up the term "double action" to know what it meant. Didn't need to be cocked to be fired, but it could be. Even the Smith & Wesson name on the barrel was filed off. This wasn't the gun of a neighbor whose wife maybe got fed up with having it in the house and ignorantly tossed it into the bushes. It was likely a criminal's gun.

I wanted to pick it up, aim it, see what it felt like to hold a real handgun. I'd shot one before when I was much younger, but it had been decades. Cuddy stole his father's nine-mil Berretta once when we were sixteen, and we drove out to the desert and shot it near a canyon. I was a pretty good shot, but so was he.

Why in a sock? Why in my yard? For how long? I was supposed to be calling the cops, turning it in. I was supposed to be doing the right thing, but then I thought of the conversation Cuddy and I had had last year on that mountain, on that rock, the Praying Monk, the day of Holly's funeral. No strong connections, no ties. No consequences. The upshot would be us walking away free and clear, no guilt, no looking behind our backs.

No one has seen me with this gun. No one knows I have this gun.

I opened the chamber—had to look online for how to do it. It was fully loaded, the bullets new, shimmering from the sunlight through the window. I tucked it back in the sock and hid it in four different places before settling on the most obvious, my sock drawer. No one would go in there. Rachel didn't do my laundry. I did my laundry.

It just so happened that evening I saw Dale out mowing his lawn and pretended to take a stroll around the block. "Hi, Dale," I waved and continued to walk, taking a chance. But when he turned off the mower, I knew immediately that I was going to find out why a gun was in my front yard.

"Hear what happened last night?" he asked, wiping his brow. "Somebody walking their dog got held up about four blocks down. My supervisor said we chased the guy right down here, past our houses, apprehended him down there at the corner." Dale was pointing down the street, past my house.

"No shit?" I said, surprised.

"Victim said he may have had a weapon of some sort, but nothing was recovered."

"Holy crap, are you serious? Jesus."

"Yeah, a lot of the time victims think the perp has a weapon, but it could have been something like a stick or a rock he shoved in the guy's back, maybe covered up with something like a bag or a cloth. No, so they found nothin on him, and he said he didn't have anything, of course. No big deal, we still charge him with armed robbery."

"Wow, so they'll like wrap a metal pipe up or something and pretend they have a gun?" I responded.

"Man, these brainless morons do all sorts of shit. They'll rob you and then hand you the empty gun, thinking that if they get caught, us cops will have a heck of a time figuring out who actually had what. They'll jack a car and try to convince us the vic let them have the car, just like that, on the street at a red light." He shook his head and waved his hands. "If the heat's on them, they'll stuff a weapon in something like a sock or a sack and stash it somewhere, go back to it another time. So keep a look out—"

"A look out for what, socks?" I knew right away that it was a dumb question.

"Keep a look out for anybody that looks suspicious or anything around the yard that seems out of place," he explained. "Hell, didn't you hear about the poor lady who was shot and killed at the thrift store in Washington Heights? No perp. Not a suicide. How do think it happened?"

Dale stood there, waiting for me to respond.

"Uh…no actual shooter, and she didn't kill herself?" I scratched the back of my head. "I didn't hear about that. What happened?"

"She was sorting donated clothing. When she picked up a sock and went to shake out the contents of it"— Dale made a pistol motion with his hand and shot it—"a loaded .22 caliber handgun hidden inside."

"*No…*"

Dale nodded. "Took the round right in the center of her chest. Dead at the scene."

"Jesus," I said.

"A tragic, accidental incident." Dale shrugged and began to meander back toward the mower.

"That's terrible. Wow. I'll let you get back to mowing." I turned and started walking again, eager to get around the corner, eager to call Cuddy and tell him I'd be driving down to Arizona with a loaded gun that had no connection to either one of us.

13

Blister

I'd rather be holding up a watermelon in the desert and getting shot at than doing this.

The shaving cream was draped across his boss's back. His hand shook when he held the razor. Always did. Cortez didn't really know why, probably from the awkwardness, probably from nerves. He ran the razor down nape to waist, frowning, then washed it in a bowl of water on the bed. He resumed the same technique, desperate to take his mind off his work.

Why couldn't he hire a woman to do such a thing for him? Pay some girl. Send someone up here to wax him off, he'd probably enjoy it. Maybe she give him a happy ending. Though el diablo would likely need to do some nasty things to her as well before his verga get hard.

"So, boss," said Cortez, "have you thought it over yet?"

"Waxing, yeah, I'm gonna have that done, but…well, this is relaxing."

Cortez closed his eyes and shook his head, knowing his boss couldn't see him. He was dreading having to do the chest next. The boss would just roll over and stare at him creepily as he shaved every hair down to the flesh between his hips.

The shit you do for this psicópata, Herman Cortez. At least he do his own pubes.

"No, boss, I'm talkin 'bout the other thing, the thing from Caborca. The guys, they mean muthafuckers, boss. They let me bring back all that stuff, and we still owe them, we owe them…like five, six more bags of cash," said Cortez. "We make a lil money off our regular stuff, but not enough yet."

"Take it easy, Hermie. This is America. We own those muthafuckers. They'll get their money in time. It's good to show some upper hand here. We've scored big so far, but we need more boots on the ground. I'm looking at the big picture here. I could become a bona fide drug dealer, like Scarface, Tony Montana. Not just some middleman schmuck still trying to set up deals for PEDs, peddling mediocre amounts of smack and crank. Build myself a real empire, you know?"

Rory turned his head briefly up at Cortez. "I could get a Gulfstream! Buy a beach mansion in South Miami, get a fuckin yacht like Tiger, a cigarette speedboat! Fuck yeah, Hermie. You know the amount of Latina pussy down in South Florida?"

What it must be like to be rich and want more. What it must be like to be rich and want to be richer and also be estúpido. How much is enough?

He finished Rory's back and toweled off the rest of the shaving cream. Grudgingly, he picked up the shaving cream can, straightened up, and quietly said, "Time to roll over, boss."

"The numbers are looking good so far, Hermie, but get Dragovic on the phone when we're done here. Like I said, we need more boots on the ground to really push this mix, first across the valley, then across the state, then, who knows, across the country, across the globe.

"Man, this is a rush! I'm stoked about this, Hermie! I should have been doing this long ago."

The razor blade neared his waist, and Cortez caught Rory looking at him strangely, as if he were willing him to cut the flesh a little.

"Sure, boss," said Cortez, gently pressing the razor back to the middle of Rory's chest. "Ya know, product needs a name, boss."

Rory looked at him curiously.

"Well, you really want to make it yours and not have it attached to the Caborca guys who, you are aware, are attached to a much bigger and deadlier cartel in Mex-ico—"

Rory nodded.

"—so you want to put a brand on it. Your own per-sonal brand. Since, you know, it is a new mix of a drug, and you did have a hand in creating it."

"I created it," Rory corrected him.

Cortez paused, waiting to see if his boss understood his actual message. Silence. Cortez continued to shave and speak.

"The H and the coke and the meth, all have the scor-pion brand on them. I just saying…you put a logo or a name to it is all, might be good for business."

"Hmmm…" Rory gently fingered the right side of his neck, a red loop stretching across it. "Blister. We'll call it Blister. 'Hey, you, want to get someone to do whatever the hell you want? Slip them some Blister. It dissolves clearly and has no taste. Blister. Get her or him or yourself Blistered! You want *anyone* to do *anything*, pick up some Blister, undetectable, untraceable in the bloodstream, Blister."

"Bleezer?" asked Cortez.

"Blister, have them stamp it on each little packet…in blue…no, in pink! Blister. Fuckin dictators from rogue countries will be buying the shit to keep their enemies at bay. It will revolutionize the way we manipulate societies. With its power to mask emotional and physical pain, people will start taking it recreationally. Who wouldn't want that? Most people think life sucks anyway. Stay on Blister and coast through your pathetic life with no pain and no fear."

"Bleez-her?"

"No, you fuckin spic, Blister! Just like it sounds." He looked down with a hopeful expression to see if Cortez had cut him a bit.

Cortez was careful and quick and knew what his boss was trying to do. It was time to change the subject, and fast. "Boss, we go shoot the M27s sometime this week?"

"Oh fuck yes, the M27s! I almost forgot about those bad boys. Fuck yes." He settled his head back down onto the bed. "Don't forget to moisturize me afterward."

14

Sweat and Tears

The road went from paved to gravel to dirt, from wide to narrow, as Cuddy steered the jeep up to a high point on the west side of a mountain. He slowed but didn't fully stop until he could see the gorge below and the dried-up riverbed. He grabbed his binoculars and zeroed in on the dirt bikers skittering across a dusty trail toward a rock formation.

"Which one are you, Rory?"

One of the bikers came to a stop by blowing up dust. He took his helmet off.

"There you are, asshole."

The other bikers came up shortly, attempting burnouts and donuts. After a few minutes, they all stood there, helmets off, drinking from water bottles. Rory sauntered around bowlegged, feigning a cowboy, drawing a handgun from his waist and shooting at saguaros.

"I'd have to take each one of them out. All four. One by one. He would have to be first, that's priority. They wouldn't know what the hell had happened to him. They'd go to him. Take another one out while he crouches over him. Now, they'll be figuring it out. Someone's shooting at us. Maybe they'd go for those guns in those bags—if they have them—maybe they'd just run crying and screaming from the blood and gore, go hide behind a rock. It'd be a little tricky if someone got to that assault rifle they like to jerk off to, got a bead on where I was shooting from. I'd stay in the jeep. Maybe crisscross the canyon, throwing them off? No. Kick up too much dust, give away where I was. I could just go down there, say I was off-roadin, lookin to do a little skeet shootin out here. 'Hey, it's a small world, Rory James.' Pull! Start blasting the shit out of all four of them.

"Bullet casings. Fragments. Forensics. Tire tracks. Cell phone pings. Say one lives, crawls to a horse trail, someone comes along and calls it in?

"Oh Jesus, I sound like Sammy Mac now!"

The heat pressed down on Cuddy's neck. He was sweating profusely and hadn't realized it. A heavy wash of emotion erupted from within. Tears and sweat covered his face.

"Fuck! What the fuck is wrong with me?! What if I don't give a fuck what happens? Put one in my own head before going to prison. Fuck! I have got to get my thoughts together…"

He punched the steering wheel. "C'mon, Cuddy, stop acting like this. Hike up there to Black Mesa and put one in the head, let the vultures pick my eyes out, tear my intestines out. Who the fuck would care? What am I livin for, anyway? To work out? To sell illegal drugs for Coach? No wife, no kids, nothin. Dad offed himself, Mom's in a home, doesn't know me from her bedpan.

"Stop thinkin like this.

"I'll think how I want to think, goddamn it!"

He fired up the jeep, jammed down the clutch, and jerked the shifter into first. "Fuck! Get it together, man!"

The tires kicked up dust and loose rock.

15

Sales Meeting

The house was full of mirrors, tuxedo sofas, plush white carpet, Hopi warrior Kachina dolls, Indian pottery, but not in the den. The den featured white walls pocked with animal head mounts—plenty of elk, javelina, mule deer, antelope, and one very large desert bighorn sheep. The den also had mahogany flooring, track lighting, a cobblestone fireplace, leather couches, and a massive rosewood desk. At the far end of the room, across from the massive rosewood desk, French doors opened to an expansive backyard of desert.

Cuddy was the last to arrive. He had walked around the adobe home and entered through the French doors. There was no space to sit on any of the couches or the two leather chairs directly in front of the desk. One guy on each of the couches took up at least two spaces. Twelve guys were present, all muscled up, some young, some Cuddy's age. Their tiny heads sitting atop large hulking shoulders like cantaloupes atop boulders.

Coach Drago, wearing a tight white shirt and dark athletic pants, stepped down into the room from an opening that led from the kitchen, his chest entering first. He was bald and tan, and veins ripped along his wrinkled skin. When he spoke, big white horse teeth jutted from his mouth.

"Okay, ladies, the reason I called this little meetin is we've been contracted out to sell somethin a little different than what we've been sellin," he said in his raspy voice. "As you all know we're gettin hit pretty hard nowadays with all the shit that went down from BALCO to Biogenesis, so we need to branch out a little. Product called Blister."

"Is it supposed to make yer dick bigger, Coach? 'Cause that's all my clients ever ask about."

"Shut up, Tommy. It's some kind of powder drug that makes people slip into a euphoric state or somethin, I was told. Don't know, don't really care. Anyway, supposed to make all of us a lot of money."

As Drago handed out packets, some of the guys squawked, some tittered, some hooted. "All right!"

Cuddy did not say a word. It was one thing to sell illegal drugs that made your body recover faster from an injury or made you perform a sport better or work out harder, but it was something else to sell an illegal drug that messed with someone's head. Holly Karlan was on his fraying mind. But he knew the rules, the game. You didn't object to selling Coach's products. You didn't object to anything Coach wanted you to do. Even at sixty-three, the man wielded a heavy hand. He'd beat you himself or order one of his men to do it. Besides, he's the one that pulled most of these meatheads out of the gutter at one time or another, including Jimmer Cuddy. There was a sense of loyalty there.

"Coach, we're to be selling this shit at the gyms?" Cuddy asked.

"At the gyms, at the bars, at the clubs, wherever you pansy-asses go to find pussy, or what you think is pussy." Coach pointed at Cuddy. "By the way, yer lookin a little fluffy in the gut, son. Might want to crank out some crunches the next two weeks, reevaluate your reps. And what's up with your eyes? Look like you've been cryin."

The men laughed at the notion of Cuddy crying, any one of them ever crying, weeping, blubbering. The thought of it was preposterous.

Cuddy looked down at his gut.

He can't even see my six-pack through this shirt. Fluffy? That's bullshit.

Still, he'd get to the gym after this meeting and bust his gut open with crunchers, maybe pop some Oxandrolone for the hell of it.

Fifty packets of this Blister he was given, to sell at a Benny per. One hundred times fifty equals five grand. He was to keep two, three would go to Coach, who would kick up a share to whomever he was receiving the product from.

Coach could sense his protégé was having misgivings. Stiffly, he waddled over, threw a burly arm around Cuddy's neck, and turned him around to look through the French doors that led out to the vast desert.

"Hey, you all right, son? You look like shit." Cuddy was aware Coach was fucking with him.

He didn't give a shit about feelings. Never had. It was coming—a slap to the back of the head or a chokehold until submission.

Cuddy looked up quizzically at him. "Do we really need to be going down this road?"

Coach fired back in that raspy voice, "Oh hell, I'm told it's as harmless as baby powder. Probably just sugar and spice. Stop being such a pansy-ass; it's gonna make us both a lot of money. I'm not sure if you realize that we need something big to hit in order to get back on track." He slipped behind Cuddy and went in for the chokehold, but Cuddy jumped and shoved him back.

All the men stood up, stunned. No one raised a hand to Coach. Ever.

"What the fuck is your problem, Jimmer?" said Coach.

"You want to put me in a chokehold, you fuckin piece of shit? I'm a grown man! Start treating us like we're men instead of your little cabana boys! And...my name is J. Cuddy."

*Oh shit, the tears. No, fuck, not the tears. Not here. Not in front of...*He spun around, looking out across the desert again, trying to focus on something, following the desert floor until it sloped upward to a road, where a truck sat with its hood up, and a man stood hunched over the engine.

Cuddy put his hands to his face to shield the waterfall, but the blubbering just got worse. He dropped down to one knee, heard the snickering, the muffled laughing. "You fuckin Sally-ass." Coach ordered everyone out. "Go sell some shit, goddamn it! Get the fuck out of here!"

The men began to file out of the room, toward the kitchen. "And hey! No mention of this to anyone! Or I'll hang you up by your balls—if you have any!"

Coach turned his attention back to Cuddy. "Oh, stop crying like a little girl." He waited for Cuddy to stand up and look at him. "You're a fuckin disgrace, you know that?" he said, shaking his head. "Always have been. Yer in your forties and yer crying like a child."

"Where you getting this stuff?" Cuddy had stopped crying, but the pain was all over his beet-red face. He held out a few of the Blister packets in his hand.

"What difference is it to you, numb-nuts, and why the hell are you acting like such a queer?"

Cuddy knew the answer. It had somehow made its way through the electrical storm in his head. "Rory James?"

Coach's voice lowered. "Now, how the fuck did you know that? You gonna leave me, start sellin for him? Is that what all this shit is about? I figured you guys would eventually hook up, knowing one another from high school and all."

Cuddy froze, trying to control his breathing, the tears, the rage. Coach took it as a sign his assumptions were correct.

"Rory James was one of my biggest clients. I started my entire operation around that kid. You think he was Mr. Natural?

"And then he sent me the bulk of my clients through his connections in the minors. Hell, shit-for-brains, if it wasn't for him, you would have never made the money you have in the 'roid and PED business. His connections in Mexico is where the fuckin synthetics come from, where the Tamoxifen comes from! Nearly all those client

prospects I passed to you over the years came from him."
He studied Cuddy's eyes.

"So, you fuckers want me out, is that it? That's fine, but I want your shit sold as soon as possible, and I want my cut. That's this shit, plus your regular rounds. All of it. And I want it soon, or so help me, I'll mount yer head up on that fuckin wall!"

Cuddy stood up. He didn't face Coach just opened the French doors and went out into the heat. He took a few steps on the patio and stopped, staring out across the desert to that slope, to that ridge, to that road in the distance.

"Sure, Coach," he muttered to himself and went around to the front of the house to his jeep.

16

You Don't Remember?

Her face drew into a scowl, a dazed and confused scowl. She seemed only slightly aware of what was happening and what had happened. Groggy. Different clothes from what she was wearing the night before: pink sweatshirt, black pants. Who put these on her?

"Did I put these on?"

A Gucci bag sat on the bed. She liked Gucci, liked Prada more. Absolutely loved Louis Vuitton. It looked like it had stuff in it, nice stuff, shiny jewelry.

Images flashed in her head, she sickened at one such image and touched her neck gently. Her throat was dry and scratchy, the skin around her neck tender.

"God damn, I drank too much again," she said to herself.

She stood but quickly sat down, clutching herself below her waist. Pain, throbbing pain. Uncomfortable, she adjusted, thinking maybe she just stood up too fast. No, something wasn't right. Everything ached—down there, up around her shoulders, her thighs, her wrists, ankles.

What's his name? Cory? What had they done?

She didn't want to think about it.

He's rich, Gabriela, look at this bedroom. I could get used to this. Maybe I'll have his baby.

The extravagance of the bedroom took her mind off the throbbing. She wanted to call her girls and tell them about this bedroom as big as their apartment. She wanted to tell them she wouldn't be coming home for a while, she wouldn't be at the salon for a while.

Where is this Cory? What are we going to do the rest of the day, the rest of the week, the rest of the month, the rest of the year, the rest of our lives?

She adjusted her bra. Something was irritating her nipples. Finally, she pulled the cup down. A hole, clogged with dark dried blood. She pulled the other cup down, put her hand under her breast and lifted it up to get a closer look. A hole, clogged with dark dried blood. Something had been put through both nipples. They were pierced.

A chain…I think.

She tried to remember, but the effort made the sore spots throb. Feeling dizzy and nauseated, she lay back down yet tried to recall the man she met at the club.

Nice hair, nice eyes, nice body. Very nice car, silver Mercedes, with a driver. Even had his homies in an Escalade following us. Yeah, I could get used to this.

Rory James sauntered into the room wearing nothing but a black silk robe, collar up around his neck. He smiled; sat on the bed.

"Hey, baby, that was a lot of fun last night. Listen, I need to get to work, so I'm going to have to ask you to leave soon, but I'll hit you up later, and maybe we'll go have dinner sometime next week." He looked her over. "You feelin' okay? You seem a little out of it."

Through the haze, she could see the bags under his eyes and the form of a devious grin, but he seemed genuinely concerned, and that was nice. He was leaning over her, looking into her eyes. Maybe he was going to kiss her. Maybe he'd want to have sex again.

They for sure had sex, right?

She didn't think she could have sex for a while, with the soreness down below and everywhere else. She noticed the expensive watch on his wrist. She'd power through if he wanted to, maybe even blow him, despite feeling so groggy.

"I really had a great time," she said, "but you know"—showing surprise, she continued—"I'm really not feeling too well and…it's really strange but I'm sore like…everywhere." Gabriella said it as if she was embarrassed, but she was more embarrassed that she couldn't remember this rich guy's name and what they had done the night before. "What did I have to drink? Did you put these clothes on me?" She put her hand on her cheek and smiled.

Rory continued to grin. "You don't remember? Yeah, well, you had a lot to drink. Listen, you take your time. Why don't you throw on a bikini and sit in the hot tub for a while, maybe that'll help. And help yourself to anything in the kitchen."

She thought he was going to lean in and kiss her, but he just kept grinning. He stood up and headed for the bathroom.

As she timidly rose from the bed, the pain down below grew more apparent.

17

The World of Make-Believe

*W*hen did I lose my willpower? Did I ever really have a backbone? Stand up, Sam. Be a man. Now is the time. Now.

"So, I'll be taking off in the morning. First thing. Gonna be a long, lonely drive."

Rachel turned her head his way, raised her eyebrows, tilted her head. "Did you say something?" She had been reading a book in bed. "I'm in the middle of one of my stories, Sam."

"Yeah, I'm leaving in the morning, probably about five. Might drive straight through." He smiled with the possibility that it might ease any tension. It never did. What was the point?

"I thought Mike and Peter were going with you." She went back to the book.

Perfect. Here comes the lie. Be a man, Sam. Really sell it.

"Didn't I mention it last night? They both backed out yesterday. Mike said he caught hell from Gwen, and Peter said Toby has the flu." He looked at her and noticed she wasn't really paying attention, engrossed again in her book. "I don't think either one of them really asked their wives or really wanted to go in the first place." He moved around, adjusted himself, pulled a magazine from the nightstand. "Oh well, football tickets are bought, Cuddy's expecting me. I'll just...Rachel? Honey?"

She put up her hand and kept reading. He hated when she did that. It was so demoralizing. But he waited. And waited. Staring at her. Her hair, too short, too fake yellowish. It was hair you'd see on a little boy. Her plump cheeks, almost a double chin. There was a cute face in there at one time, long ago. Maybe. He waited.

Finally, the hand went down.

"What is it?" she asked.

The same ole Sam, backboneless Sam.

He reached under the covers and put his hand on her thigh. "You wanna?"

"What? Why?" She looked appalled.

"Because I'm leaving tomorrow morning, be gone a few days. It's been...what's it been..." Sam looked up at the ceiling, pretending to figure. He knew it had been five, maybe six, fuckin months.

What married couple goes five, maybe six, fuckin months without having sex? Five maybe six nonfuckin months!

"...maybe a few weeks or so?"

Reluctantly, Rachel closed her book. "Well, I guess, okay." She studied him for a moment. "Did you shower today?"

Sighing, Sam replied, "Yeah, I showered."

He sidled up next to her while she seemed to brace herself for something she didn't really want to do but knew she had to. She leaned back, putting her arms between the two of them. The arms were supposed to go around him, but he didn't broach the subject. He gently kissed her chest, went to move up toward her mouth, but she lightly pulled his shoulders back down to her cleavage. From there Sam moved to slide her pajama pants off. When he started to come back up to her chest, she stopped him by putting her hands on his head and guided him down to her crotch. He paused for a moment, disappointed, and then went in between her legs. Rachel closed her eyes and kept both hands on the top of her husband's head. Every couple of seconds, she'd adjust his position by manipulating the angle and the rhythm.

Sam hated this, too. Not the act itself, but Rachel's involvement in the process. He stopped and looked up at her. She forced his head back down without opening her eyes. After a while, she let go a shrieking moan, and Sam thought for sure she was trying desperately to muzzle herself from saying someone's name. He moved up, tried to slide in but she took ahold of him with her left hand.

"I want to put it inside you, Rachel." It sounded thin, adolescent, even whiny.

"No, this is fine," she said. Her eyes were open now, and she was looking past him, off somewhere, jerking away.

"Could you not yank so hard then? Jesus," he begged.

"Well, come already, it's getting late!"

She took her hand away as his face tightened, and he dropped his head into a pillow, letting out a muffled moan.

"Damn it, Sam, you got some on my hand!" She got up from the bed and went directly into the bathroom, slamming the door. He lay there, face in the pillow, breathing heavily, unsatisfied.

By the time Rachel got back into bed and turned off the light, he was already drifting off to the night with Holly. They were getting out of the taxicab, her arm wrapped around his. It was an old apartment building, only a few floors, and people, mostly male Mexicans, were out milling about a small courtyard, even at the late hour. Holly nodded to a couple of them, and they nodded back. But that's not the part Sam focused on. He didn't picture the filthy apartment, the drug paraphernalia on the coffee table, the empty beer cans and bottles on the floor, the dirty sheets draped over the windows. He didn't see the steps he took through the trash, the half-eaten fast food and the strewn clothes on the frayed couch, because none of it was in this reflection.

He saw Holly, only Holly. Her silky black hair, her slippery blue eyes, her soft mouth smiling at him. She was holding his hand so delicately, leading him through the shadows cast by a single dim light in the small apartment. She wasn't pulling or tugging or mindlessly jerking him off. He could stop her at any time, but he had no reason to.

"Don't look around, Sam, this place is only temporary until I can afford to get out of here, maybe buy a car and go to California."

"I don't care to look at anything but you." He's not sure if that's what he actually said, but it worked for this purpose. Besides, it was like a line from a movie. She turned with that and brought him in. They embraced and kissed, and he gracefully lowered her down onto a bed.

***

It was a wonderful night. But it didn't end like a fairy tale.

I'd never made love to a woman like that before in my life. It was intense, and we were both in sync with every move, with every kiss, with every touch. Nothing was done in haste, nothing was done with a deadline in mind. Eyes were open, attentive to every sensation. Everything was done with enjoyable patience. Holly would smile at me, and I'd smile back, kiss her, and her arms and legs would tighten around me. I studied all her tattoos, from the pistols across her lower back to the beautiful monarch butterfly on her lower abdomen.

The room was hot, and we were sweating, forming damp outlines on the light blue sheets. We would briefly stop, only to smile again or to catch our breaths, but then we would start back up. In my ear, Holly would softly moan my name. I'd caress her breasts, her legs, anything I could get the tips of my fingers on while the motion continued. She seemed to really drink that in, the tenderness. It was as if she was surprised by it.

"I've missed you, Sam McElroy," she whispered, and the embrace tightened.

The climax was simultaneous. At least I think it was. Our bodies stiffened, and our mouths fell open, and the past was forgotten. There was no guilt, no bitterness, no remorse.

Afterward, we held each other, like it was young and new, like we had all the time in the world. I wasn't tired.

In fact, it was the exact opposite. I felt rejuvenated. We talked about our lives. She talked about California again, moving there, but not to the traditional California, not the coast. She wanted to go somewhere like Lodi. She really loved that song John Fogerty wrote. *Oh Lord, I'm stuck in Lodi again.* Seemed like Lodi, California, was a place for lost souls. And you had plenty of choices.

"You can wake up in the morning and decide whether to go to San Francisco, San Jose, or Sacramento, all depending on how you feel," she said. "Doesn't that sound great?"

It did. Having and making choices made a difference in your general outlook on life. Some choices turn out to be mistakes, some don't. We were lying side by side, naked, wrapped in a sheet. I moved a strand of hair from her face, kissed her, and she smiled.

"Sam McElroy," she said. "Here you are."

That's when I could see the past rising up in her eyes and slipping down her cheek. I wiped the tear, but another came, and another, until we were both crying and holding each other. I wanted to finally make everything better for her. She didn't deserve this life, to live like this. She knew I wanted to try to help her yet again, and I think she was maybe emotionally taken by the persistence of it, the devotion.

Maybe...this...is...love. I don't think she knew enough about it, and it scared the hell out of her. Holly had no idea how she made me feel at that moment—purposeful, alive. Or maybe she did.

She sat up and looked at the sheet across the window. Dawn was breaking. She reached over to the nightstand and lit a cigarette. She was beginning to shiver. I sat up and lightly caressed her naked back, running my fingers along the pistols, the roses, the barbed wires, along the bone of her spine.

"Three hundred," she said, sniffling, looking away from me.

"Three hundred what?"

She didn't look at me. She kept her eyes on the window, blowing smoke into the burgeoning light.

"Three hundred a night. It'll cost you more if my alcahuete, my chulo, Omar, comes home."

It was registering. "Holly—"

"He doesn't like seeing the perdedores I bring home. But he likes seeing the dinero, and if the dinero ain't there, and he knows I was shackin up, then he won't let me get high. And I ain't sure which is worse, not getting high or Omar's wrath."

"Why don't you get off the stuff, get away from here?"

"It's what keeps me alive, Sam. Low doses, between the toes. Strippers don't look so appealing with tracks down their arms. It's what keeps me safe and warm." She couldn't turn and face me.

I wanted to say: We can run away. Go to California or someplace else. Get intense treatment, wean you off the stuff. You could come to Chicago. I'd leave Rachel, remain in Elsa's life. You'd probably make a cool stepmom with the tattoos. We could make a life. Here I go again, twenty-something years after proposing the first time. Weren't we meant to be together?

But I knew it was the world of make-believe.

"Three hundred cash," she said again. "You got it on you?"

I did, but I told her I'd have to go to an ATM. I wanted to give her more, whatever I could pull from the machine.

"Omar's hombres outside will follow you to the corner store. He's a member of Las Cuatro Milpas street gang. They'll take more than the three hundred if you decide to run." She paused. "If you're thinking about leaving more than three hundred, just know you'd be giving it to Omar Rosales, a gangbanger, and not me." She blew smoke from her nose. It wasn't Holly anymore. It was a tattooed-up, middle-aged junkie-stripper-prostitute. "And I'm not a charity case, Sam."

I got up, put on my clothes, ripped all the cash from my wallet save a twenty for a cab—it was more than three hundred—and put it on the bed in front of her. I went over to her phone on the nightstand and typed in my number and name, just S-A-M. She would not look at me. But I leaned on the bed and put my face in hers.

"You want to start over, you call me. And Holly, what we have is as good as love."

She was looking down, her head buried in her knees. I kissed her on the top of her head then walked out of the bedroom.

I could hear her crying as the front door closed.

18

So Far Gone

The rising sun, somewhere in the east, thinly spread a red-and-yellowish glow across the Phoenix sky. Sam cut the engine of his little four-door red Fiat. Rubbed his face. It was an effort to get out, his legs and back stiff. He stretched and cursed, had to piss. Cuddy wasn't going to like being woken up, but what the hell.

Took ten minutes of knocking before the front door of the townhouse slowly opened. It wasn't Cuddy but a young woman, half-dressed, holding a pillow over her bare chest. Silk-looking pajama bottoms.

"Who are you?"

Sam shook his head and grinned. She was cute, dirty-blond hair, small facial features. The pillow was having the time of its life.

She's gotta be half his age. Same ole Cuddy.

"I'm Sam, a friend. I bet he's sleeping?"

The young woman sighed, "I wish. Guy's a machine, rarely sleeps."

Shirtless and in cargo shorts, Cuddy appeared behind her. His face lit up when he saw Sam. "What the fuck! How the hell are you, bro?"

As Cuddy hugged and slapped him on the back, Sam was surprised by his friend's jovial demeanor and warmth. Cuddy seemed jacked up on something.

"C'mon in, man!" he said, smiling, bouncing.

The young woman glowered. "How can you have so much energy? You're acting so crazy."

Cuddy hadn't stopped smiling. "I know, baby, but now I need to catch up with my old friend, so go catch some Zs. I'll check up on you later." He pointed upstairs, his index finger twitching.

Sam put down his suitcase. "I tried calling you from a pay phone in Amarillo and again in Flagstaff, but neither call would go through," he said, yawning. "Pay phones are hard to come by these days."

"What the hell is a pay phone?" asked the young woman as she lumbered up the steps, the pillow slipping lower and lower.

Cuddy and Sam looked from her body to each other. "Precious," said Cuddy. "But seriously, why didn't you call me on your cell?"

"I didn't bring it. Left it at home," said Sam as he headed for the bathroom.

"Forgot it?"

"Nope. Didn't bring it," he called back from the hallway.

When he returned to the living room, Cuddy was sitting, one knee shaking intensely. He bolted right up at the sound of Sam's voice.

"Why are you so chipper at six in the morning? You high or something?" Sam asked.

"No, I'm just feeling great. I'm in a great fuckin mood, a great fuckin mood. I can't believe I feel this way. I don't even know, but it's great. I'm glad you're here. Shit, my place is a mess. I been runnin round. Met this girl, I think…somewhere…she called, and I told her stop on over. You wanna go grab a bite?"

Sam fell onto a couch and put his feet up. He hadn't noticed how messy the place was, and it hadn't registered how strange Cuddy was acting. Too foggy from the lack of sleep.

"I need shut-eye. Drove straight through. No cell phone, no tollways, no GPS. Nothin."

"You're off the grid?" belted Cuddy with a grunt. "What have you come here to tell me, Sammy Mac, what have you come here to do? What are we gonna do, brother?"

"Let's talk…" Sam was mumbling now, his eyelids drooping, "later. Let me…sleep."

***

He was groggy, slipping from unconsciousness to consciousness, hearing unusual noises and then hearing nothing. He thought he heard the young woman who was at the door earlier yelling about something. It was faraway but loud. He thought he heard whimpering, but then it faded. He rolled over on the couch.

Cuddy having a fight with this girl?

Sam drifted back to sleep.

It was early evening when he finally awoke. He sat up to a quiet house.

"This place is a disaster," he said aloud. "Jesus, Cuddy, get a cleaning service or somethin."

The front door was wide open, and thick, warm air was filling the foyer. He closed the door and heard whimpering, coming from Cuddy's room upstairs. The door to the bedroom looked closed. He picked up his suitcase and started up, figured he'd give a listen at the door when he walked by on his way to the guest room.

What's he doing, breaking up with her?

He stood silent at the door. It was only partially closed. Sam had a bad feeling. Maybe this wasn't a breakup or even an argument. He tapped it open.

The room was as messy as the rest of the house, clothes, shoes, trash, bongs, newspapers, barbells, pill bottles everywhere. The white drapes that covered the open sliding glass door of the balcony billowed from a breeze. The whimpering continued. It was coming from behind a closet door. Tentatively, Sam approached it. He turned the knob and pulled it open. It was a walk-in, and it was dark. He opened the door more to let the light in, and then he saw him.

His best friend, his life-long friend, the tough and buffed-out former Marine who had killed probably members of the mujahedeen in Iraq, who had beaten the shit out of guys twice his size, who scaled mountains and banged young hot women, was curled up in a fetal position, his hands over his head and face, sobbing like a child.

Sam rushed over and squatted down next to his friend. "Cuddy, what the fuck happened? You okay? What are you doing in here?"

Cuddy startled, swiped at the wetness on his face, and shook his head. He blinked incessantly to clear the tears and focus in on Sam. He forced himself out of the curled-up position.

"What? Oh, shit, I…I just been havin…well, you know, I been havin…" His face burned red, and a vein jutted from his forehead and streaked down into the corner of his left eye socket. The flow of tears became more pronounced again. "…a real hard time with everything lately…I don't know…just a lot going on." He seemed to be willing himself out of it. Standing, wiping the tears, catching his breath. "I'm…fine. I'm…all right."

Sam patted him on the shoulder. "C'mon, pal, let's get out of here, go downstairs. You can tell me what's going on."

"Yeah…yeah, I'm okay. I just slipped into a real dark place."

They made their way out of the closet, Cuddy turning back to glance at the camouflaged rifle on the shelf above them.

They went down the stairs and sat in the living room. Cuddy's leg was twitching again.

"Did your friend leave?" asked Sam.

"Yeah, I guess she did."

"What was her name?"

"I have no idea," replied Cuddy, and with that they both laughed, breaking up the awkwardness.

"What's going on with you? This isn't you. You're a goddamn mess. Your place is a mess." Sam wasn't sure how to approach it. Cuddy stared at him for a few seconds, that vein settling back into his forehead.

"Well, where to start, really: hows about last year I was diagnosed with both bipolar and post-traumatic stress disorders—"

"By a doctor?"

"No, by the Dalai Lama—Yes, by a fuckin doctor. Right around Holly's funeral. Was having horrible nightmares, mood swings, intrusive thoughts, flashbacks to my time in the military and to Holly's night, the works. One week done in by so much self-loathing, the next week riding high on life and its possibilities. I remembered my mother mentioning that term 'bi-polar' after my father offed himself. Figured, you know, I ought to go in."

"Yeah? And what did they say?"

"Come to find out only a small percentage of PTSD symptoms appear many years after a traumatic event. They put me on Lithium. But I've tried a little of everything, Valium, Xanax, Ativan, to find some sort of a balance. Sat down with a shrink more than a few times, too."

"Yeah? And how'd that work out?" Sam went to nod and admit the question was stupid, but Cuddy interrupted.

"I stopped taking the drugs, and I stopped going to the psychiatrist. It's my past. I can't escape it. My father—who, you're more than aware, really wasn't a father, just a man on the floor with a bullet in his head—the thing with Holly, guys in my fire team getting their bodies blown apart, Coach and his shit…there's no escaping such things."

"But why did you stop the drugs and stop seeing the psychiatrist?"

"'Cause I don't give a fuck anymore." He looked away, either trying to hold in another sobbing session or a raging temper tantrum.

"You can get really fucked up trying to live that way, Cuddy," said Sam. The statement held no weight. They both knew it was already at that point.

"Coach is having us sell a new drug called Blister, and his supplier is none other than…wait for it…"

"What does that have to…Rory James?"

"There it is."

"Jesus Christ."

"No, probably more like the devil. Does the devil have a name?"

"Rory James is selling drugs through Drago?"

"I told you last year I thought maybe he was still at it, raping women. Anyway, I'm not selling the shit, and I'm gonna let Coach know I'm done with all of this. No more selling anything illegal. Nothing."

"You're not still using?" Sam was sure Cuddy was, looking at his cut arms, cords of veins in the biceps and forearms.

"No, figured it was a bad combo with the mental meds trying to fend off the mental wounds." Cuddy took a deep breath. "So, now that you know all about how fucked up I am, tell me what the hell you had to drive all the way down here to tell me or show me or whatever."

Sam didn't know if he should even bring up the .38. Maybe this wasn't a good time. But life wasn't all peachy for Sam McElroy, either. He was miserable, just as Cuddy always suspected. To make matters worse, here he was driving twenty-four hours straight from Chicago to Arizona to give his best friend an untraceable gun so he could kill a guy they both despised because of what the guy did twenty-five years ago.

Who's the mentally stable one in the room?

"I didn't mention this last year, but I think, or I'm pretty sure, Rachel's having an affair."

Cuddy grimaced, his face showing true disgust. "With whooo?"

"I think this guy she works with. George."

"Poor guy."

"Yeah, it's been…been difficult for me."

"No, I'm talking about this George, asshole. He's got to be more screwed up in the head than me to want to do anything remotely even resembling having sex with your wife. Oh, god, the thought of it makes me queasy."

Nearly a minute passed as they stared solemnly at each other, Sam's arms folded across his chest. Finally, they both grinned. Sam broke the silence. "Are you sure you're mentally unstable? Because you sound a lot like you always have, givin me shit."

"Maybe I've always been unstable. And maybe your wife truly is a fuckin bitch you should have never married and had a kid with." Cuddy moved to the end of the chair, rested his elbows on his knees, and looked at Sam sternly. "Now, what are you really doing here?"

Sam jumped in, told him all about the .38, how he came into its possession, how he was thinking this would be a perfect situation where the gun had no connection to either one of them. He pushed some trash aside and put it down on the glass coffee table next to a pair of binoculars. He was trying to gauge Cuddy's interest but couldn't read his friend's expression.

"It's loaded?" said Cuddy halfheartedly, only eyeing it from a distance. "You should be careful. Could shoot your balls off."

"I've shot a handgun before," snapped Sam. "Remember the Berretta?"

"Oh yes, we shot the same gun my father shot himself in the head with."

Sam gave him a dubious look. "Seriously?"

Cuddy nodded. "Only gun he had."

"Jesus, the hits just keep coming," said Sam. "You know, I'll get rid of this." Sam reached across the table and picked up the .38, "and spend the next few days getting you and this dump of yours cleaned up. You've got a lot on your plate right now and this…well, this is just gonna make it worse."

"Put down the gun, Sam," Cuddy said sternly. But his friend just stood there.

"But—"

"Put it down."

Sam put the gun back down on the glass table and sat on the couch. He was spooked by Cuddy's cold glare.

"I can't close off the other parts of my past," said his friend, "but at least I'll be able to close that part off for the both of us."

Sam spoke soft and rigidly. "Are you sure, Cuddy?"

"I'm sure."

***

Sam ordered some food. Cuddy only wanted more beers, a scotch or two. He needed to chill. He went to the minibar and poured himself a single malt. He picked up the bottle, studying it.

Talisker. Coach's favorite. Why the fuck do I drink scotch? A sixty-dollar bottle of whiskey.

When he came back into the living room Sam was on his laptop pulling up Google Earth and checking out the mountains beyond Carefree, Arizona. Sam spoke for a while, mentioning the measly .38, but finally Cuddy chimed in.

"I don't mean to burst your bubble here, Sammy Mac, but we ain't gonna need that .38." He held up his hand to stop any ridiculous protest from his friend and took a sip of his drink. "I understand your thoughts about not having connections that can get traced back to us, but all I need is my huntin rifle, somewhat of a level surface, and the right conditions, and I can take care of that prick no problem. Hell, I've told you about the bighorn sheep I shot dead with Coach and a guide a few years ago?"

While rolling his eyes, Sam nodded a yes. He'd heard the story from Cuddy several times, but here it came again.

"I was lucky to get the draw, and we found one finally on our ninth day, out feeding in a small cut shielded by the wind. After a four-hour stalk, I shot it from four hundred-plus yards out. Man, it was fuckin raining and windy. Took another six hours to skin, quarter, and hike back to the trailhead."

Cuddy was picturing it in his head. "Coach was beside himself, had it mounted in his den because he paid for the tag, the guide, the gear. Whatever...I shot the beautiful creature. He didn't give a shit about that, just wanted the trophy."

"The cops will look into all of Rory's associates, but they'll thoroughly check out the ones he may have had criminal dealings with, including Drago, which may or may not lead to you. That's risk. There should be no risk."

Cuddy didn't look his way. He took a hefty sip of the scotch. "When you want something bad enough, Sam, there's always risk."

The night drew on, Sam doing most of the talking and Cuddy doing most of the drinking and toking. Sam's words—his opinions, his scenarios, his schemes, his strategies—became a dull drone in Cuddy's ears. He'd grunt or shrug when asked his take on a possible idea, just to get Sam off his back.

There's no sense in talking to the guy, explaining it. He wouldn't get it.

He was relieved when Sam finally stood up and yawned.

Before he went to crash in the guest room, Sam asked Cuddy again if he was sure about all this, considering, "You know...the state you're in."

Cuddy didn't answer, just lit a joint, nodded, and waved him off.

Sam looked down at the pistol and back at Cuddy. "But I can trust that you won't do anything stupid?" He wanted to take the gun with him back to the guest room, for safekeeping. *Cuddy was suffering from some pretty bad shit that he didn't know too much about, but he wouldn't kill himself. Would he?*

Cuddy blew marijuana smoke from his mouth, nodded, and waved him off again.

***

Hours later the living room was dark and smoky. Folk singer Joe Purdy was singing a song called "Wood Box" in a constant loop on the laptop, a slowly picked guitar ringing out. The rifle, a camouflage Remington R-25, was loaded, pointing up, the stock on the floor. Cuddy was sitting, holding it between his legs with both hands, one on the barrel, one lower, near the trigger gauge. He was staring at nothing out before him, his eyes dull, his face solemn, hard-boned. He hadn't slept in days. Sleeping brought the nightmares, the chills, the pain. Why sleep?

His best friend was here now. Somewhere. He didn't know for sure anymore. It didn't matter anyway.

That .38 on the table, that's gutsy for old Sam Elliot McElroy, Mr. Straight-and-Narrow, married with a kid, working an honest job. Knows nothin 'bout the criminal world.

Cuddy admired the man, admired his moxie. Sam was never one to lose control.

Now, thinks he has it all figured out.

Cuddy didn't have the heart to tell him he could have gotten any untraceable gun for the job, probably could have scored a few Tec-9s, for cryin out loud. Didn't need him to do the job, period. Could leave him out of it altogether.

Feel sorry for him, though, guy's got nothin but this one thing to get him out of bed in the mornin.

The anguish fell upon Cuddy in droves.

You get so far gone, there's nothin to pull you back.

Over the previous days and nights, some female friends of his had left messages, wanting to see him. He'd get an urge and let one or two in, just to try to fuck the demons away. Coach had left several messages, demanding he go on his sales calls, to get him his Blister money.

"Hey, cocksucker, they say you haven't been at the gyms. There are customers to feed, you little prick! Get off your ass and make your rounds! I got people calling me up the ass. You remember what I told you, you little cocksucker."

Inside J. Cuddy's head, images formed: Buddies smiling, training, laughing, grimacing, barking, running, jumping. In their dress blues, in their combat fatigues, in their civilian clothes. In a fight. In a shit storm. In a bloodbath. In a body bag. In a coffin draped with the US flag. In the ground.

He's running, firing, hollering. He's diving, digging into the desert. Explosions. Bullets. Blood. Body parts.

Fingernails can't dig a hole in the desert for a man to crawl into.

Stairway. Bedroom door. Rory's evil smile. Sam's indecisive, distressed look. White bed sheet. Holly's naked body. Bloodstains.

Cuddy leaned forward, tilted his head back, placed the barrel into his mouth, the tip pointing up toward his brain, a mass of frenetic confusion. *Gotta do it right.* He reached his right hand down and...just before popping the trigger with his index finger...

Inside his head, images formed: Holly's desperate facial expression in that shitty motel room. The urn being lowered into the ground. Mrs. Karlan weeping in the Arizona heat. Rory James standing at the front door of his mansion, the young, confused girls walking down that winding driveway to the waiting cabs. Coach and Rory doing business. Blister packets. Cash. Doped-up women. Sam McElroy, his friend, left alone to finish this tragedy. Sammy Mac. Rory James, that sinister look.

Rory James.

Cuddy pulled the barrel from his mouth, stood up, swung the rifle up onto his shoulder by its sling, grabbed three bullet magazines off the table that were sitting next to the .38, and was...out the door.

19

Long White Bow

At the top of the stairs there was a white door, and through that white door was a bedroom, and in that bedroom was a large brass bed and a naked teenage girl passed out.

It was our friend, Holly. We had hesitated to open that door. We both knew she was in there. We both saw her go in there. We saw Rory James leading her in there, his hand holding her hand, Holly giggling, stumbling behind him. "What, Rory, what do you want to show me?" Later, we saw Rory come out of that room.

They had been dating a few weeks. It didn't bother me. I was happy for her. She was ecstatic. He'd stand by her locker waiting for her to get her books for the next class, and off they'd walk together. I remember thinking that was nice, the way he waited for her like that. Knowing him, I figured he'd make her wait, maybe even have her carry his books. But I remember thinking maybe I didn't really know him, even though we had grown up together. Maybe, deep down, beneath all that arrogance he was a nice guy. She was happy, anyway, but she wouldn't talk to me about it. I think she just kind of thought that I'd get jealous or something. I was a little jealous to be honest, but I didn't let it show, and it made me happy to see her so happy.

It was funny how things were changing. The three of us were still close, myself, Jimmer, and Holly, still talked to each other, still gave each other rides home from school, but things were changing. Jimmer had moved on quickly from his father's death. I wasn't surprised that he would. His father was always a no-show at everything family or Jimmer related. I'm not even sure Jimmer ever had a meaningful conversation with the man. I know I never did. After he died, Jimmer stopped coming over as much. There was a time he'd be at my house watching television when I'd come home from someplace. Just hanging out. It was fine by me and by my parents. There was no question he'd stay for dinner, too. But after the old man's death, I guess he felt he could hang out at his own house more.

Anyway, he caught a ride with me over to Karen Preston's party. She was having a two-kegger, because her folks were in Bermuda or something, and they gave her and her younger sister free rein of the house for four days. It was a great party. I didn't drink but one beer, because I had driven over, but Jimmer was into the sauce pretty heavily, scouring the place for girls. The music, an assortment from U2 to the plentiful hair metal bands, was up high, and some girls were dancing, and some boys were playing quarters on a glass table. Some people mingled, others formed circles, standing there talking in little pods. All the types were there. That's what made it such a great party. The popular kids, the geeks, the mods, the losers, the dweebs, the jocks, everyone seemed to put aside their differences for this one particular party. Maybe it had something to do with it being early in the school year, or maybe it was because we were seniors and already starting to grow out of all that bullshit.

I saw Rory open the screen door off the back patio, Holly following him. He entered like he was gracing the place with his presence, chest out, lips curled up, thumbs tucked into the front of his jeans. Holly was holding a red cup and smiling. She was greeting her girlfriends, who seemed to be more locked in on Rory than Holly. When she passed me, she only glanced over and gently touched my shoulder. We didn't have to say hello to one another. Our relationship was beyond that. A glance was all that was needed. We'd known each other too long. Her glance said, "Hey, stud." And my reply with my eyes and a nod of the head said, "What's up, girl?"

When I saw Rory's face after that intuitive exchange between friends, I felt that pang of awkwardness that always emerged when he and I locked eyes. He didn't like me. Never had, even when we were in grade school. He never liked anyone except the person who was complimenting him. He knew Holly and I were good friends and lived down the block from each other, and he didn't like that either. I don't know, but he gave me sort of a menacing look that night and then grinned as if he knew something I didn't, or he had something I didn't have, or was going to take something he thought I wanted. And then some guys started high-fiving him and telling him what a great game he had recently pitched in the high-school playoffs.

"You'll be in the bigs before long, Bro!" one of them said.

Holly looked good that night. She was wearing a denim miniskirt and a thin white blouse. The outfit made her look sexy, but the long white bow in her dark hair made her look…cute, adorable, precious. I had never seen her with her hair pulled back in such a way. It made her innocence that much more palpable.

It was a warm night, so most of the girls weren't wearing much. And they all looked good. You could say we teenage boys were in a frenzy. Stuff was going on in some rooms upstairs, in the corners, in the shadows out by the pool, away from the patio lights. I'm pretty sure there were some kids in the hot tub as well. Jimmer was trying his best, as always, but with no luck. When I saw him standing by the stairs drinking, he waved me over and asked what the deal was with Holly and Rory James.

"I think they're an item," I said.

"That doesn't bother you?"

"No, why would it?"

"Uh, because the guy's a complete fuckin douche bag, moron?"

"I don't know, maybe he's not all that bad. He's always been a little arrogant, sure, but maybe you have to be that way in order to be a star athlete. It's probably been hard for him to fit in over the years. We should cut him some slack. She seems really happy."

Just then they appeared out of the throng of teenagers, Rory pulling Holly through the crowd. As they split between Jimmer and me, Rory turned and gave me that menacing—almost vengeful—glare again, while Holly smiled, took a big swill from her red cup and hollered,

"Jimmer and Sammy, my boys! Woo-hoo," over the music.

They went up the steps, and we watched them go. When they reached the top of the stairs, that's when Holly was giggling and stumbling a bit. Rory turned around and whispered something into her ear. "What, Rory, what do you want to show me?" she asked, giggling more affectionately.

And they went through that white door. Jimmer looked at me with a stone-cold expression. A lull in the music had ended, and I yelled through the din, "C'mon, man, get another beer and have some fun. It's a party!"

Karen Preston and I were talking about colleges in the Midwest. She was considering the University of Iowa, and I was looking at Loyola in Chicago. If we ended up at those schools, we figured maybe we'd try to meet up sometime. She'd come to the city, and I'd go out there for a Big Ten football game. Karen was nice to everyone. That also may be why so many different walks of life were at that party—because Karen was so nice to everyone. Her boyfriend, Tony, was thinking about going to Texas, which was causing a rift between them.

Anyway, Jimmer walked up and yelled in my ear. "I need to talk to you!"

I followed him up the stairs, and we stood in the hallway in front of that white door.

"They're still in there," he said solemnly.

"Jimmer…"

"Shutup."

"You gotta relax. Holly's a big girl. She can take care of herself."

"You're a real prick, you know that?"

"What do you want to do? Bust in there? And then what?"

"You think Holly is cool with this…with what may be going on?" Jimmer looked mortified and a little drunk.

"Hey, she went in there; she can walk out of there if she doesn't like what's going on in there."

Just then the door opened, and Rory was standing there adjusting his jeans at the waist. He looked up at us as he closed the door behind him. "You want sloppy seconds, muthafuckers?"

That's when my heart dropped into my gut.

He didn't…he didn't just have sex with Holly, my Holly, at a party and then walk out of the room and leave her lying in there. You don't treat your girlfriend like that. You don't treat anyone like that. You don't treat Holly Karlan like that.

Before I could say anything, Jimmer threw down his cup and shoved Rory, but the guy barely budged. He grabbed Jimmer by the neck with his left hand and slammed his head into the drywall, leaving a perfect indention. I jumped between them and pushed both away from each other with my hands extended. "Whoa, whoa, whoa, guys, it's cool, it's cool. Just chill. Just chill."

"I'll put your little body through that wall you ever touch me again, you little shit!" said Rory.

"Fuck you, asshole. I ain't afraid of you," Jimmer shot back, but he wasn't trying to push me aside to get after Rory. That knock to the head had either jolted him pretty good, or he had sobered up real fast and realized who he was up against.

Rory watched us both as he went down the stairs, shaking his head. "You three are fuckin pathetic," he said. "She wasn't even worth the effort."

We stood there in front of the white door only seconds, but it felt like a lifetime. And then Jimmer went into the bedroom first. I don't know why, but I stayed in the doorway.

Holly wasn't in there. The big bed had a bulky comforter on it. At first I think we both figured she was in the bathroom to the left of the bed, maybe crying, maybe cleaning up. But then the comforter moved a little bit, and Jimmer rushed over and pulled it back. She was naked except for her miniskirt pulled up around her waist. There were splotches of blood on the sheet between her legs. She seemed in a daze, out of it, rolling her head from side to side and mumbling. Jimmer sat down on the edge of the bed next to her. I quickly stepped into the room and closed the door. I don't know why I felt I needed to close the door. I think it was because she was lying there naked, and there were people all over the house, and maybe I didn't want anyone to see her naked.

"Holly, Holly, you okay? It's Jimmer." He touched her right wrist and her face. I walked closer to the bed.

"Jim, pull down her skirt, so it's not showing," I pointed between her legs. Jimmer threw a scowl at me, and I felt horrible for suggesting it, but I didn't know what to be saying or what to be doing. I didn't know what was happening, or what exactly had happened.

He reached over and covered her again with the comforter. And then she mumbled it. She mumbled it, but we both heard it plain as day.

"Where were you guys? I…I called for you."

She didn't say it harshly. It came out soft and pleasant, but maybe only because she was in such a daze. The one streak of tear that ran down the corner of her right eye confirmed something terrible had happened. Jimmer leaned in closer to her face, and I stepped closer to the bed. I wanted to hold her and tell her it was going to be okay. I wanted to tell her we'd go back an hour or so and change everything to how it was—and this, whatever this was, we would never let it happen.

"Did he hurt you, Holly? Did he hurt you?" Jimmer asked, because you have to remember we were teenage boys, not everything registered black and white.

She looked up at me, her face forming into a little pout as she started to cry. Jimmer leaped up, "I'll kill the muthafucker! I'll kill the muthafucker!" He bolted for the door, but I jumped in his way and stopped him. He was little then, so I could stop him. He was little, but his eyes were on fire with rage. I'd never seen them like that before. His whole face turned a dark reddish hue, while those eyes, man, those eyes were like brimstone. Scared the shit out of me. I thought briefly about stepping out of the way but changed my mind.

"Wait, wait, wait, hold on!" I lightly shoved him back and closed the door. There was a chair near the door, and I jammed the top of it up under the doorknob. I didn't want anyone coming in and seeing Holly like this.

"Get the fuck out of my way, Sam!" He came at me again, arms flailing. An elbow caught me right on the tip of my nose.

I pushed him back. "Just wait a minute! You don't want to go do something stupid!" Our hands and arms shoved and slapped at each other.

"Stop! Please stop!" It was Holly, and she was sitting up now, holding the comforter to her chest and crying intensely. She folded in her arms and dropped her head into her hands, letting out short wet sobs, that long white bow in her dark hair bobbing.

Jimmer went to her side. "I'll get him, Holly. I'll make him pay. I'll fuck him up beyond all recognition. I promise you. I'll do it. I'll break every bone in his body."

She was still in a daze. She raised her head and moaned and dropped back down on the bed. "Nooo…nooo…" she mumbled, while moving her head from side to side. "Stay with me, please. Stay with me, Sam."

She was reaching her right hand out at Jimmer. He took it, looked at me, that malice in his eyes. "Get the fuck over here!" he whispered. He instantly turned back to Holly, "We're here, baby. It's going to be okay. We ain't going anywhere."

She curled up. I sat on the other side of the bed and put my hand on her shoulder. "It's okay, Holly."

"Sam's here," affirmed Jimmer.

She reached back and put her hand on mine. She was holding Jimmer with her other hand. "I feel sick," she mumbled. "I feel really sick." She started to sidle off the bed, at first slow and then hurriedly. Jimmer stood back and let her go, her naked self slipping from under the comforter and rushing toward the bathroom. As she vomited, I thought we should go get one of the girls, maybe Karen Preston, to help her, to stay with her while we called the police.

Jimmer looked at me from across the bed and pointed. "I'm gonna kill him. I'm gonna kill him."

Just as I began to tell Jimmer my idea, Holly called out, "Sam!"

Timidly, I followed Jimmer into the bathroom. She was on the floor curled up, a strand of the long white bow stretched across her naked shoulder. He knelt down next to her. "C'mon, Holly, let's get you back up in the bed."

"No," she said sharply, her eyes only half-open, streaks of tears everywhere down her face. You couldn't see the sharp blue of those eyes at all. "I need, I need to wash all this off. Put me in…" She motioned toward the tub.

I felt I had to say something. "Holl, we need to call the police. I'll get Karen, and maybe she can help you get dressed—"

"No, no, Sam. Please. Please just help me first, Sam. Please…" She was begging, still in a stupor, but begging. It was a heartbreaking plea that I knew I'd never forget.

Jimmer stood up, carefully shimmied her denim miniskirt down past her feet, then walked back around her and put his arms under hers, his hands brushing past her breasts. I'd never seen her naked breasts before, and I wanted to keep looking at them, and I didn't want to keep looking at them. I felt ashamed when I gawked at her breasts and at the hair between her legs, which looked to be bristled in dry blood. I put my hands under her knees, and we lifted her up and gently put her down in the tub. Jimmer turned on the water at the faucet, but she motioned for the shower spray. And the water came down on her as she rested there, lying on her side, her head tilted with the upward slope of the fiberglass.

She didn't look like she wanted to move, but she let out a heavy gasp and a cry and turned over on her back, allowing the water to fall on her chest and everywhere else. She was crying intensely again, looking up at the ceiling, the tears flowing down her face and her neck into the pooling water. Jimmer knelt down beside her, beside the tub, and she took his hand. She turned her head toward me, weeping uncontrollably, and I knelt down, too.

She spit out the word "soap" in a soft childlike squeal. Jimmer placed a bar in her hand, but it slipped out. He didn't even hesitate when he picked it up and began soaping her himself, rubbing it over her thighs and hips and waist and chest frantically. I grabbed a washcloth, plunged it in the accumulating water, placed it on her belly, and gently put her hand on it.

She looked up at me, those blue eyes as dim as a moonless night's sky. "I'm sorry," she sobbed.

As Jimmer soaped, Holly and I washed, all three of us weeping and working together.

At one point I noticed that long white bow floating in the water.

***

Sam reached down and picked up the bra and handed it to Holly. It was capri blue and had lace in it, he noticed that right off. She put her arms in it and balled up the back of her hair. He knelt down on the bed behind her and hooked the back of it. Before she let her hair flow back down over her back, he noticed deep red hand prints on one side of her neck and one streak of red on the other. He knelt there examining the marks. Now the image formed in his head: Holly on her back on the bed. Rory over her, one hand clenched around her neck, the other pulling up the denim skirt...

"Can you hand me the rest of my clothes?" she said quietly, and it snapped the image from Sam's head.

The panties were the same color as the bra, and Sam picked them up as cautiously as he had the bra. He saw instantly that they were ripped, one side perfectly torn. He grabbed the blouse and the skirt and put them on the bed in front of her.

"These are torn," he said ominously while crumpling up the panties and placing them on the bed.

Holly nodded heavily before taking the skirt under the comforter and pulling it on, and then slipping into the white blouse. She edged herself to the back of the bed to lie down. Sam sat next to her and leaned over, his head next to hers.

"Can we call the police now?" he whispered.

She turned her head away, and he could hear her crying again, sniffling against the pillow. Jimmer opened the door holding a glass of water, and a wave of loud music burst into the room. He quickly closed the door, put the chair back up against it, and went to the bed, sitting on the opposite side.

As she took a sip of the water, Jimmer explained to Holly that he had told Karen Preston that he and Sam were taking care of her because she had drunk too much.

"I don't want to call the police, Jimmer," she said in a muffled tone.

Jimmer's eyes darted up at Sam, who grimaced and mouthed, "What?"

"Just rest for now, Holly. Just rest. Your mom thinks you're spending the night here, right?" asked Jimmer.

Holly nodded.

"Just rest," he said again and took her hand.

"You guys aren't leaving me, are you?" She turned back to Sam, holding out her other hand. He took it.

"No, no. Just rest," he told her softly. "My folks think I'm stayin at Jimmer's, so we're not going anywhere. But we should…"

Jimmer shook his head at Sam, no.

They were both sitting up, leaning against the headboard on opposite sides of her, each holding a hand as they watched her drift off to sleep.

After a few hours or so, when the dull sound of the music had stopped for good, and the house seemed quiet, and the boys had dozed off a few times only to awaken, startled by the slamming of a door or a loud shout from a rowdy partygoer, Sam woke up and leaned across Holly and tapped Jimmer on the shoulder. His friend blinked his eyes and focused.

"Don't we need to be callin the police?" Sam whispered.

Jimmer looked irritated. "We don't need to do anything," he whispered back. "She'll tell us what she wants us to do."

"We're sitting in a crime scene, Jimmer! We can get in a lot of trouble for not reporting something like this. Jesus, the guy strangled and…and"—he didn't know if he should say it—"raped her! He needs to be arrested, go to jail, man! And she should be at a hospital."

Jimmer seemed to consider the words for a moment but then looked down at Holly, who was sleeping peacefully. "It's whatever she wants us to do, Sam." He looked back up at his friend. "We wait."

In the morning, Holly woke first and sat smiling at the two of them as they rubbed the grogginess from their heads and faces. When they finished and looked at her, their expressions grim, it registered what had taken place the night before, and her smile disappeared.

"Oh, no," she moaned and began to cry. "No. No. No. Oh, no. Oh god, no."

20

Una Sonrisa

It was a glorious smile, cheeks raised, mouth closed, lips stretching into sunken dimples. Chest was out, both hands behind his back as if standing at attention. Eyelids fluttered. He tried the doorbell again, redid the capacious smile, sucked in all the air to again bump out his massive chest. Oh, he was feeling…what was it?

Virtuous!

Faintly, he could hear the deep bass sound of electronic dance-club music coming from somewhere deep inside the mansion.

Surprisingly, there was no rage ripping through J. Cuddy's veins, no wicked images flashing in his head. There was only a warm, beautiful wave of clarity.

The man talking on the intercom sounded Mexican. "Yes, who is it?"

With maybe too much ebullience, Cuddy replied, "It's Jimmer Cuddy and I'm here to see Rory James."

"Mr. James is uh…preocupado. You friends with Mr. James?"

"I've some unfinished business with the man."

"It's late, amigo, what you got business with Mr. James this late for?"

Cuddy tightened up that smile even more and turned his head up toward the camera in the corner.

"Rory, I assume, is torturing the hell out of some girl right now, and she can't do anything about it because she's looped up on a drug called Blister, and if you don't let me in to wait out this disgusting habit of his and talk to him, then I'll turn around and drive straight to the local sheriff's office…Comprende, *amigo*?!"

"Sí, Sí, I let you in. You have any weapons on you?"

The smile widened more predominantly, perhaps giving away a little secret. "No, sir."

"I no believe you."

"Well, there's one way to find out, amigo. Open the door and frisk me."

Y Inside the little room, no bigger than a closet, off to the left of the expansive foyer, Cortez was moving his eyes around three different monitors. One showed the front of this large, muscular hombre standing erect in camouflage cargo shorts and black tank top at the front door. Another showed a blue open-top jeep parked in the turnaround next to the water fountain outside the portico. Another showed the quiet, winding stone driveway down to the main road. Cortez fingered his moustache, contemplating.

"Show me yer hands," Cortez said into the speaker-phone on the desk.

Cuddy raised both his arms out to his sides. The barrel of the Remington R-25 rested behind his upper left leg, the butt of the gun on the ground behind his left boot. The brilliant smile hadn't left his face.

Cortez motioned to Hosk, who was walking out of the game room holding the Glock he had gotten from behind the bar when the doorbell rang.

"Where de ladies?" Cortez asked Hosk.

Hosk nodded to the game room. "Messed up," he replied and grinned.

"Put the gun away and open de door," Cortez said.

Hosk put the weapon in the front waistband of his pants and went to the door. He turned the gold deadbolt, pulled open the big oak door, and smiled at the man standing there.

"Howdy!" said Cuddy, beaming.

When Hosk went to nod at the cheerful man, Cuddy grabbed the barrel of the Remington and flung it up, catching it with both hands and pointing it at his face—all in one swift motion.

"No!" yelled Cortez watching the monitor from the closet room as the shot rang out.

The bullet snapped Hosk's head back violently, blowing off a section of his skull. His legs began to buckle, but before they gave out, Cuddy was already inside and swiping the Glock from the dead man's waistband and shoving it into one of the pockets in his cargo shorts. The body hit the marble floor as Cuddy turned toward the small room off the foyer. Cortez had kicked the door closed and dived under the table that held the monitors. Cuddy blew two large holes in the door, one high, one low.

He felt elated, a profound euphoria he hadn't experienced in years.

It was dull now due to the gunshots, but he could still faintly make out the electronic dance-music coming from up the stairs. Impulsively, he began moving in that direction while changing out the expended cartridge in the Remington with a new one.

Four bullets in, two mags at the ready. That closet is not clear, but that muchacho is probably shitting his pants. Some things you never forget.

He was halfway up the stairs when another man appeared in the foyer brandishing a shotgun.

"What da fuck? Cortez!" T-Ray hollered desperately as he leveled the shotgun up at the guy standing on the staircase.

The wall exploded over Cuddy's left shoulder, and he felt a sting in his neck, followed by a warm substance on his skin trickling down his chest and back.

Still, it all felt exhilarating.

He made his way down the stairs firing at the man, filling him with four huge holes, all in his sternum.

Bull's-eye. Bull's-eye. Bull's-eye. Bull's-eye.

One shot would have been well enough, but Cuddy was feeling frisky. The man backed up against a wall and slid down, smearing his blood along the way.

"Cortez!" shouted Cuddy near the bottom of the stairs now. "I know where you are, amigo. Now answer me." Slowly, methodically, Cuddy began to make his way back up the stairs toward the music, again replacing a magazine.

It's like being out on patrol all over again!

"What is it?" came Cortez's muffled voice from inside the little room.

"How many more in the house besides you, amigo?"

"Podría ser veinte…"

"Twenty? You're full of shit, Cortez. I'm gonna guess I'll find what I'm lookin for up here."

"They's plenty of cash and drugs in de grande room, plenty of pussy in de game room, too, if you want it."

Peering down a long corridor, Cuddy found the door where the music was emanating from and moved toward it. It was at the end of the hall, white light flashing through the space at the bottom. He took one last look down at the foyer below before focusing on the door.

"You sit tight, Cortez, and you may make it out of here alive."

"Sí, señor."

***

Rory raised his leathered head up, listening. He thought he heard something that went beyond the blaring music. He looked at the door and then back at the girl spread out naked on the bed, her wrists and ankles tied down with leather straps to each bedpost. Creamy white skin, red hair, the youngest Rory had had in a long time. Her eyes were open, and she was smiling up at him, in a stupor.

"Hermie! You bringin another, or what?"

He stood there with nothing on but the leather mask over his head and face, no hair anywhere on his naked body. He held his penis in one hand and a riding crop in the other, waiting. Cortez was supposed to be bringing in another girl, the feisty Croatian. She had taken a while to sedate. The hog-tie kit was out, and the chains hung from the beam on the ceiling. This was going to be two for the price of one, or something like that. Maybe more. Rory didn't care, as long as it got the job done. He looked back at the girl. Strobe lights flashing. She was petite and pale, except for a thick orange bush of hair between her legs.

Rory moved over to the stereo system and switched the music off.

"Hermie!"

No answer.

"Cortez, get your ass in here! You need to shave this bitch down before I do anything to her!"

The door blew open, and Rory turned, startled. He let go his penis and dropped the riding crop. The flashes of light showed a large man aiming a very large rifle at him, bearing down on him.

"Get on your knees!" yelled Cuddy, placing the barrel at Rory's head. Cuddy's eyes shot from the leather masked man to the naked girl on the bed to the chains hanging from the ceiling and back to the leather masked man. The flashes became irritating, igniting a spark inside his head.

Rory was belligerent, throwing his hands up, dropping to his knees. "Who the fuck are you! Who the fuck are you! Oh god, please don't kill me, don't kill me. I didn't know she was your daughter, your girlfriend, your sister. Please, please, I have money, lots of money. Bags full of cash. Don't shoot. Don't kill me. Pleeeease!"

Cuddy had gone tense, breathing heavily, beads of sweat forming on his brow. That smile and feeling of euphoria had suddenly been replaced with a scowl and a feeling of gloom. He could sense the wave of anxiety rising up.

Stop the flashes.
Stop the chaos.
Stop the begging for your life!

Bombs were going to explode in his head. He could sense them falling from above, men were going to die in front of him. He lowered the Remington, grabbed the Glock from his pocket, flipped it in his hand so the barrel pointed at him and the handle faced the man with the leather over his head and face.

"Take it, Rory!"

Rory looked up, his eyes glassy. "What?" he squealed. "Why? What are you gonna do?"

"Take it, Rory!"

Rory reached for the Glock, gripped it with his left hand, and pointed it down.

"Now yer gonna put it to your head and pull the trigger," said Cuddy, the damn bombardment closing in. The strobe flashes more alive, ripping through each iris.

"What? No, I can't do that…I—"

"Do it, you piece of shit!" Cuddy raised the Remington back up, aimed at one of the open slits of the leather mask. "Do it!"

Shaking, Rory moved the gun up to the left side of his head. More squealing. "First…first tell me, tell me who you are!"

"Corporal J. Cuddy!"

"Cu…Cuddy? Jimmer Cuddy? But why, why do you want me to do this?"

They had arrived, the bombs, exploding all around him. The flashes of light had stopped, only the images flashed incandescently now: his father on the floor, Holly in the bed, his buddies in a heap. A hole smack dab in the center of Coach's skull.

C'mon, Cuddy. One more set. Stay…frosty.

"Do it, or I'll do it for you."

The command was followed by a splashy pop, and blood sprayed across the pale girl and the white sheets of the bed. Rory's head hit the hardwood floor as Cuddy toppled over him. Cortez was moving into the room, pointing the Bushmaster rifle at the pile of men on the floor, trying to get off another round before the big dude rose to his feet.

Cuddy groaned, clutching the left side of his body and reaching for the rifle that had fallen out of his hands and slammed against the floor, the scope breaking off. Rory scurried out from underneath him, kicking, slapping, squealing. He stood up, his naked body mottled with blood.

"No, Cortez! No! I got this!" He aimed the Glock at the back of the head of the mutherfucker who was down on all fours, struggling to get up, and pulled the trigger. Cuddy's body hit the floor with a thud and he died instantly.

"HOLY FUCK H-CHRIST!" squawked Rory, jumping up and down, his white teeth shone in the gap of the leather facemask. "HOLY FUCK H-CHRIST! THAT WAS UNFUCKING-BELIEVABLE! HA-HA, WOOO! YES!"

No, it can't be, thought Cortez, lowering the Bushmaster to his side while staring at his boss through the flashing white light.

Una sonrisa.

He can't be…he can't be smiling.

21

Luck of the Draw

Ⅱll four shots had missed their mark. In between each, somebody spit out a command in a harsh whisper: "Raise the gun up! Steady it! Get the barrel off the ledge! Get the fuckin barrel off the ledge!"

On the last shot, a twig from a dried-out tree had snapped from the bullet and landed on the animal's nose, spooking it and making it dart from a ridge out of sight.

"Fuck! You worthless shit-for-brains! You call yourself a fuckin hunter!"

Cuddy was seething quietly, waiting for the hammer to drop even more. Coach was burning holes into his head, he could feel it. Then, Coach finally spoke again.

"What the fuck is wrong with you, boy? You get me this once-in-a-fuckin-lifetime opportunity, and you blow it by resting your barrel on the fuckin rock? You stupid fuckin piece of shit! I taught you better than that! Everybody knows you rest your barrel on a rock or a ledge it's gonna throw off your sights! You worthless inbred!"

The guide, Walter, a stocky older man originally from Texas, tried to ease the tension. "Hey now, Mister Dragovic, mistakes they get made out heres all time. It ain't mean the hunt is up. You ought go easy on him now. They'll be another shot, soon enough."

With that, Drago stood up from his crouched position beside the rock and whirled around to face the guide. "You mind yer own fuckin business. My five grand don't pay to hear your advice on what I can say to this queer-uva-pussy-inbred. If you and yer lazy-ass outfit would have tracked the damn things in the fall, maybe it wouldn't have taken us four fuckin days to spot one!"

"Now, now, Mister Dragovic, four days on a hunt for desert bighorn sheep sure ain't long atall. And they's plenty of time yet to track us anotha. No need fer y'all to be so epset. Hail, he'll get hisself one—uh, he'll get hisself one for you, I mean."

Cuddy was reloading his rifle. He wanted to thank the guide for sticking up for him, but he knew Coach would think it weak and blow another gasket. As Coach went stomping down the slope to where they had placed their gear, Cuddy looked up at the sky. It was darkening to an iron color. There was dampness in the air, the desert floor seemed eager for it.

"Is yer pop always sech an a-hole, son?" asked the guide, who was looking through binoculars out where they had spotted the ram. Cuddy turned to him, replied, "He's not my pop," and gathered up his rifle and started down the slope.

He knew this was a big deal for Coach. The man had put in for a bighorn sheep tag for as many years as Cuddy had known him and never been selected. They were highly coveted tags, and not many were given out per year. This particular year only two were doled out. Whoever was lucky enough to get selected had a year to bag a ram, and with hunting season running only the month of December, it sure put the pressure on you. Not to mention, the state of Arizona only allowed each hunter one desert bighorn sheep in a lifetime. Some hunters draw on the first try—lo and behold, like Cuddy—some never do—yep, Coach Drago.

So here was Drago out in Unit 44 B South in western Arizona, the draw that Cuddy had shockingly received, living vicariously through this boy he had turned into a man, a man he had carved and molded into a younger version of himself. A man he was so fuckin disappointed in!

"I'm beginning to understand why your father put a gun to his head so many years ago." Drago was hefting on his backpack over his camouflage jacket. His face gnarled as he looked up toward Cuddy. "He couldn't bear the piece of shit he had created!" He stomped off. "Fuck!"

Cuddy ignored him, rambling down the slope and swiping up his backpack, falling in behind Coach as he started off down a trail toward the ATVs. It was the worst insult of them all, but he had heard it so many times before—especially after getting booted from the military—that it no longer made him incensed. He figured he was numb to it.

The guide called down while navigating the slope, "Looks like they's a storm may be brewin up. We may want to hunker down." He eventually fell in behind Cuddy.

After several spotty storms that caused havoc on the men but blessed the dry desert for the good part of four days, the weather cooperated enough for a hike into what Walter "gar-ron-teed" was a known territory of bighorn sheep. He was praying so, anyway. He couldn't take another day of this big crusty sonebitch berating this big younger sonebitch. It was irritating.

Coach wasn't so sure of the territory and complained about the direction the entire hike, mumbling about money and time spent and wasted, mumbling about how the stupid piece of shit rested the barrel of his gun on the rock and probably missed his chance for a ram. He finally stopped mumbling when Walter said, "Got a small herd of 'em, maybe five, up yonder high on that there ridge." The guide lowered his binoculars and pointed.

Drago took a look and immediately sighed. They were far off and high up. Probably be a few hours' hike before they were within range. He looked at Cuddy. "You better not miss this time."

For the next three hours the men stalked through fifty-mile-an-hour winds and sideways stinging rain. Finally, Walter, looking through the binoculars, leaned over to Cuddy and whispered, "Les duck down through that there brush and head up that there draw to try to gauge whether they's a big daddy or not."

Cuddy nodded. Coach Drago asked, "What the fuck did you say?"

Walter shushed him and pointed toward the brush. They made their way to within 450 yards or so of where Walter had spotted the small herd, and Cuddy unshouldered his rifle, went down to his belly on somewhat flat ground, brought the stock of the gun up, and gazed through the scope. There were just two rams now, but one much bigger than the other. The rain and the wind were relentless.

"Too much wind, scope is splashy, too," Cuddy whispered.

"Quit your fuckin complainin," barked Drago. "For chrissakes, give me the rifle!" He reached for the gun.

"Afraid I caint let yis do that, Mister Dragovic," whispered Walter harshly. "You take his rifle an hit one them sheep, y'all have to answer to the Arizona Game and Fish Department. See friend, I's a reputation and a business to think 'bout."

After a long, rain-pelting moment, Drago took his hand off the rifle, and Cuddy went back to peering through the scope. Walter maneuvered himself in between the two men, thinking it would possibly lighten the pressure off the shooter, the poor kid.

There in the scope wasn't a stalwart bighorn sheep but Cuddy's past creeping up into the sights.

First, it was his father's lifeless body on the floor of a bedroom, a pool of blood forming around his head.

Then, it was Holly's naked body under the comforter, the blotches of blood on the bed sheet.

Then, it was Coach telling him in the high-school weight room: "Well, if you don't hunt, and you aren't into fitness, then what are you into? Well, we'll have to get you into those things. You got a daddy? I had a Daddy sort of, too. Boy, I'm gonna teach you how to be a man. I'm going to get you big and strong. You're going to hunt and enjoy scotch. You're going to be a real man."

Then, it was the exploding head of an Iraqi mujahedeen soldier.

Then, it was all the blood and body parts of his Marine comrades.

Finally, Cuddy saw the bighorn sheep in the crosshairs.

Three or so minutes passed before Walter, peering through his binoculars, whispered, "Yer 'bout four hunred twenty-plus yards out. Got that darn northerly wind, a-course, and we losin daylight by the minute. One on the right looks to be a daddy."

Drago broke in with, "Don't you miss, boy—"

The shot rang out. The animal jolted and then stumbled a few feet before falling over.

"Direct hit," said Walter. "Nice shot, son. Real nice."

"He didn't fall off the fuckin ridge, did he? I don't want those fuckin horns damaged," snapped Drago, trying to spot the animal through his own binoculars. "If you shot him off the ridge, I'm gonna tear you a new asshole."

"No, them horns are fine, Mister Dragovic," said Walter. "He settin there waitin for us to come take stock of him. But he looks as near as big as a damn Texas steer from here. Yes, sir, I think you got yerself a good one, son—uh...gentlemen."

***

Walter had reckoned it was that of a nine-year-old Arizona Mexicana desert bighorn ram—and wow, to bag such a creature on the ninth day of the hunt in such blustery, rainy, and darkening conditions!

"You ought to be proud, son," he had said to the young man before snapping a photo of Cuddy and this Mister Dragovic in front of the young man's...uh, their kill. Drago had held up the head by the animal's horns and smiled for the first time in ten days. Walter tried to get him to acknowledge the young man's shot, but he was too engrossed in the animal itself. Walter was just as baffled by the young man, who didn't stand up and say, "I shot this here bighorn sheep, damn it, not you." The big young man just seemed glad the big old man was pleased.

It really got to Walter when, after he had finished cutting and field dressing the sheep with the help of the young man, this Mister Dragovic insisted Walter attach the head to Dragovic's backpack.

"He who killed it should wear it out of this here desert, Mister Dragovic," said Walter. "It's sort of a tradition in these parts and, well, ever-where else."

That's when the young man finally spoke up. "That's all right. He can wear it out. It's his, anyway."

"Bought and paid for," said Drago, hefting the pack up onto his shoulders, looking like a two-headed beast now.

"That's a shame," mumbled the guide, "an' where I come from, just plain bad luck. But y'all do what you wish."

22

The American Dream

They here, boss," said Cortez to Rory James, who had his back to him and was sitting poolside on a chaise lounge chair sipping a cocktail. His head was resting back, and he was wearing shades.

"It's about time," he said, rising from the chair in his red swim trunks. He threw a towel over his neck and followed Cortez into the house.

"Boss, this is…" Puzzled, Cortez frowned at the big Mexican wearing all black.

Should I say his name? Should he remain nameless? Why tell anyone his name?

Renato Velasquez was not paying any attention to Cortez. He was casually studying the dead bodies in the foyer.

"Cómo se llama?" asked Cortez, who cleared his throat and asked the same question again. Maybe he'd give him a name to use.

Velasquez looked up and began barking instructions to other men coming through the front door. He had yet to look at Cortez or Rory James. The blood spatter on the wall leading up the stairs caught his attention, and he went up, stopped and briefly looked at it, and then continued up. He gestured for two of his men to follow him. At the top of the stairs, he stopped and looked down, seeing blood droplets on the hallway floor. He walked down to the master bedroom, peered inside.

"Ay, mira este," he said to the two others behind him. Both were finishing slipping rubber gloves onto their hands. They followed him into the room.

"What the fuck is this?" said Rory to Cortez.

Cortez shrugged. He didn't want Rory freaking out. "His name is Renato Velasquez. Bad muthafucker."

Velasquez came down the stairs smoothing out his thick black moustache. He was finally eyeing Cortez and Rory standing in the foyer. "You keep the products at a self-storage garage in South Phoenix, so where you keep the dinero?"

Cortez hesitated. He wasn't too surprised that Velasquez already knew where the drugs were stored until they were sold. He was cartel for chrissake.

They got an eye everywhere.

But he didn't know whether it was wise to inform him the location of the cash from recent sales. It wasn't from fear that he would take it as payment, but that he would be so enraged at how foolishly it was cared for.

Oh well, it not my money.

He answered by pointing. "In the livin room. Señoritas in the game room, too."

Velasquez glared at him, slowly moved over to the entrance to the living room, and peered inside at the duffel bags full of cash. He closed his eyes in disgust and then shook his head to come back to the moment.

"Y chica bonita," he gestured up the stairs.

Cortez nodded.

Velasquez stepped over portions of Hosk's brain matter, his boots clicking across the marble floor, his men working behind him, rolling out dark plastic tarps.

"America not so different than Mexico," said Velasquez directly to Cortez. The smile went away from his moustache. "Is the only time we clean up yer mess, gringo. A gringo like you should know how to take care of such a thing. Next time, we make our own mess."

Rory broke the tension between the two men. "Hey, man, it's cool. Yeah, we appreciate all this." He was feeling inadequate now in his swim trunks. "And we've got a good chunk of the money we owe you, of course, so the trip wasn't just cleaning up this mess. We'd like you guys to stick around, enjoy a bit of…" Rory spread his arms out, "America." Silence. "Mi casa, yer casa."

Velasquez seemed to be in awe of the size of the house. He was looking around again. "Su casa."

"Pardon me?" asked Rory.

"Mi casa, su casa, pendejo," said Velasquez.

Rory swallowed. "Oh, mi casa, su casa, pen-day-ho."

Velasquez and Cortez just looked at one another.

"The jeep outside belong to the hombre upstairs?" asked Velasquez.

"Sí," answered Cortez. Velasquez nodded to one of his men, who went out the front door.

"We gonna need a trash bag for this." Velasquez gestured at the skull fragments scattered across the marble floor. "Yer gonna clean that up, gringo," he pointed at Cortez.

Cortez nodded.

Velasquez took a deep breath, turned around, and headed for the front door. Rory and Cortez followed. "Sí, long drive back," he said. "Maybe we do stay here a night or two. See what like to live the American dream."

23

Broken Glass

It was odd that Cuddy had left his cell phone sitting there, next to the .38, next to the trash, the half-eaten food, the empty beer cans, prescription bottles, the binoculars. No one goes anywhere without a phone. It was a perfect time to call Rachel, though. I was going to use his phone anyway, since I intentionally left mine sitting on the dresser at home. I just felt there was no need to be carrying around a tracking device with what I had come down here to give to Cuddy. Heck, I even avoided all toll roads with cameras or receipts recording where my car was or wasn't. Just being cautious, I guess.

I figured Cuddy had gone out to get some breakfast or to Drago's place to tell him he was quitting the business. I hadn't seen him really eat anything the night before—just kept drinking. He assured me he was okay, that he was on track, had a purpose now, was going to beat this mental disease, after, of course, this one thing was done, after we closed this one chapter in our lives.

Rachel's phone went to voice mail. "Hi, honey, it's me. Hey, I left my cell phone, of all things, on the dresser. Not sure how I did that…Anyway, I'm here. Drive was long, but I made it. I'll give you a call later. Okay? Love you."

It was midmorning, perhaps she was in a meeting or something, couldn't get away. I texted Elsa: Hey, it's Dad. In AZ. Left cell at home. My friend's phne. LVM fer Mom. C U soon!

Elsa texted back: Ma tk day off. Tld me 2 stay Steph's 2nite/2morrow and thru wknd. Said neded lone time. That's cool, but WTF

A part of me wanted to jump back in the car, drive straight home, and catch Rachel in the act. A part of me wished that young beautiful friend of Cuddy's would stop back over, somehow find me irresistible, and allow me to bang her brains out. Which I could, bang someone's brains out. Nah, I probably couldn't.

I didn't want to think about what was going on in my bed at home today, tomorrow, or all weekend. I didn't want to think that some asshole was banging my wife where I sleep, where I live, eating my food, watching my television, probably toggling through my cell phone. I didn't want to think that the two of them were going at it right then as I was leaving a voice mail. I didn't want to think that Elsa actually knew the real reason her mother had told her it was okay to stay at a friend's house the next few days. But I'm sure she did.

I only wanted to get back to the distraction at hand: Finding a way to kill Rory James without any connection to Cuddy or myself.

But where the hell was Cuddy?

I hung out at his place a few more hours, well into late afternoon. He had gotten a couple of calls from some females, but I didn't pick them up—just looked at the names: Samantha and Amanda. Lucky guy. After a while I went through his phone, scanning the photos. There were plenty of Cuddy flexing his muscles and cavorting with hot bikini-clad women at a pool, and plenty of Cuddy flexing his muscles and cavorting with hot women in spandex work-out gear at the gym. And there were plenty of Cuddy flexing his muscles and hanging out or hunting with Coach Drago, although Drago was never smiling. They were smoking cigars and drinking some kind of hard liquor in one. In another, they were at some kind of muscle-mania trade show, showing off their wares in a booth. In another, Drago and Cuddy were sitting in camouflage attire on a mountainside, and Drago was holding up the head of a bighorn sheep between them. Drago was smiling in that picture.

I went to his contacts menu and scrolled down, looking at the names. Coach Drago's was there. I thought about calling but kept scrolling. Holly's name was still in there, had her cell phone number, and Cuddy must have added the name of that shitty motel he had once dropped her off at—where she died. The Borgata. Rory's address was in there, too. Suddenly, I really wanted to find Cuddy and get this thing on its way.

I called the number Cuddy had listed for Drago and only got a voice mail. I decided I'd take a drive over there, maybe check out Rory's place, too, get a better idea of what we were up against. I'd bring the .38 with me just in case.

***

I rang the doorbell a few times, a rolling chime, but no one answered. There was an old cream-colored Cadillac Eldorado parked in the driveway. It looked similar to the one Coach Drago used to drive back in the day, but if it was the same one then he must have had the thing rebuilt. The style was the only thing that was old. The paint job was immaculate, the rims and tires brand-new. There was no rust anywhere to be found. I even peered inside. Plush interior. It was hard to believe Coach Drago still tooled around in such a dinosaur after all these years. It was a dinosaur back when we were in high school. Now it was a fossil, but it seemed the perfect fit for that loudmouth prick.

His house was nice, too, large white stucco that stood out in the dry brown desert. At one time it was likely a spec home for what became an undeveloped subdivision. The roads were finished with white curbs, but the lots were empty except for ragweed, chollas, and stakes jutting up from the ground. It wouldn't be surprising if Drago was in on this deal long ago, with it either going belly-up or reaping a heavy profit before he got out from under it. More than likely, the latter.

There was a stone walkway on the side of the house that looked as if it went clear around to the backyard. Figured I'd take a gander. Maybe Cuddy and Coach were having a serious discussion about his departing, didn't want to answer the goddamn door.

There was a stone pavers patio back there with a built-in fire pit, grill, and minifridge. It was a nice setup.

One could lounge in a wicker chair under a large canopy and look out across the vast desert. I stood there for a moment looking over the ground, wondering why Coach never put in a pool and walled up the backyard like everyone else in Arizona. Probably had something to do with his love of hunting. He could walk out those French doors and take a pot shot at a diamondback or a hyena, then go pull out some dumbbells and curl for a few hours, feel like a man. What a schmo.

As I walked through the patio and made my way over to those French doors, I noticed a shard of glass sticking out in one of the small window squares of the door.

Broken glass?

I stood on a step and peered in, at first feeling the cool air of the house mixing with the outside heat against my face. Red splatter on a white wall below the mounted head of a...I surmised it was a bighorn sheep.

I followed the red splatter downward to a man sitting at a ridiculously big desk. His head was craned back, mostly resting on the top of the backrest of a chair. His eyes were open and staring blankly at me, at the French doors. There was a large hole in the middle of his forehead and a few strands of dried blood down his face to his opened mouth. Suddenly it hit me what I was looking at...

"Holy shit!" I stumbled backward, coming to rest on a low wall. I sat there for a moment catching my breath, reviewing what I had just seen and what I needed to do next.

That's Drago. He's dead, been shot right in the center of his forehead.

Is someone in the house? Is Cuddy in there some-where…dead…alive? Do I run to the car and get the .38 out of the glove box? Or do I get the hell out of here?

Something drew me back to the French doors, back to the broken glass. I had to look again. I put my face in the jagged space. The lights were on in this room, track lights lit up bright along the ceiling. The animal heads and then the bloody bald man's head and face. I felt sick and stepped back again. Turned around and squinted into the sun, looking out across that quiet desert.

I could only make out a small road in the distance.

Cuddy could have made that shot. If he did, what else did he do last night?

***

By the time I made it up past Carefree, into the mountains, and found Rory's place, dusk was settling in. I coasted past the entrance to the winding drive, peering up at the house. Cuddy was right. It was a big mansion, complete with a water fountain at the top of the hill. I drove farther up the main road and pulled off on a nar-row dirt trail, grabbed both the .38 and the binoculars, and got out. I had to move fast to not lose daylight, so I dodged the boulders and the chollas until I was looking down on the house, albeit from quite a distance.

I felt a deep pang in my gut the second Cuddy's jeep fell into the binoculars. It was parked on the other side of the water fountain, the back facing a long portico that led to the front door, the front of the vehicle facing to-ward the main road. There was a black Suburban truck parked in the roundabout.

I maneuvered the binocs over toward the house, trying to close in on any open windows but couldn't catch anything.

What is he doing in there? Does he need my help?

Just then a man came out the front door. He was short, Mexican, wearing jeans and a blue T-shirt. He looked to have rubber gloves on. I trained the binocs on him. He opened the back gate of the jeep and walked back inside.

This isn't good. This. Is. Not. Good.

I drew the .38 from the waistband at the small of my back, but I didn't know what to do with it, so I laid it on a rock. I was faraway. The heat was letting up, but I began to sweat more profusely. The muscles in my forearms ached as I kept the binocs on the front entrance. Another man, another Mexican. This one massive, wearing dress slacks, black dress shirt, black sport coat, black cowboy boots, thick black hair slicked back. Thick black moustache. He was directing by pointing, pointing at the jeep, pointing at the Suburban. More men, three or four, all wearing those gloves. They went from the front door to the jeep back to the front door, looking as if they were studying dimensions.

This isn't good. This. Is. Not. Good. That's Cuddy's jeep, Sam. No sign of Cuddy, Sam. This isn't good.

I glanced at the pistol but went back to the binocs.

The big Mexican dressed in black slowly walked out from under the portico and stood in front of the fountain. He latched his thumbs on his belt buckle and surveyed the area, looking down at the main road, beyond that at the widespread valley desert far off in the distance below. Then he turned his head in every direction, peering around at the hills and rock cliffs above, behind and off to the side of the house. He seemed satisfied. I didn't think there was any way I could be seen, with how far up I was. He walked back to the front door, pointed and…Four men emerged from the home carrying something wrapped in a dark tarp and bounded with bungee cords. It had the outline of a human body. They struggled with the cargo, finally reaching the gate of the jeep and shoving whatever it was into the back.

They went back to the house and emerged again with another load. This one took five men, and the big Mexican in black. No Rory James. They heaved the load atop the first tarp. One Mexican, the little one in jeans, went back to the house and emerged dragging another load. This tarp had dark stains on it. When he got to the gate, he nodded at one of the other men, who picked up one end of the tarp and helped him shove the load farther in. They slammed the jeep's gate closed, jostling the loads in the back.

The short man hurried back inside and then back out, carefully carrying a rifle and a black trash bag. He made a space for the rifle to be lying flat behind the front seats of the jeep. Grimacing, he tucked the black trash bag between the…bodies.

I couldn't take it anymore. I dropped down under the boulder where I was crouched and sat in the gravel and dirt, my chest pounding.

What do I do here? Cuddy's dead. But who are the others? Is one Rory James? Who are these guys? Cartel? Fuck!

Cuddy went in, shot Rory dead and maybe an acquaintance. Or did he take two out from afar, and they found him and the jeep and took him out? Was he outgunned?

Like seeing Drago's drained skull through the broken glass of that French door, something compelled me to get closer to what was going on down there at the house. Maybe close enough to hear something.

I picked up the pistol, put it in my waistband again, flung the binoc strap over my head. I squatted low and moved swiftly to another boulder, dodging the cacti, loose rock, and the scrub. I did this a few more times until I came to a ridge that was within fifty or so yards of the driveway.

The sun was going. A jagged strip of rust ripped through the sky above. I could hear the cowboy boots on the tile inside the portico now. They crackled, the noise bouncing off stone and rising in waves up the hill. I was close enough, probably too close.

I inched above a rock—didn't need the binocs anymore to see two men standing in the portico. To my disbelief, one man was Rory James. He was wearing red swim trunks and had a towel wrapped around his neck. He hadn't changed much physically, just older skin. I felt like grabbing the .38 from my waistband and rushing down the slope firing at the cocksucker. The other man was the big Mexican in black. Their voices echoed clearly right up to where I crouched.

"Las señoritas we'll take care of," said the man in black to Rory.

"What do you mean…you don't mean…you…do you mean you'll…?"

"No señor, we not in the business of killin señoritas. Pablo take home, leave them with mucho dinero, yer mucho dinero. They go muy feliz." He paused, looking at the jeep. "If not, then we kill them."

"What…what are you gonna do with…" Rory pointed at the jeep.

The man in black waved his arms nonchalantly. "Ah, you lucky, cuz we have access to an industrial crusher and an industrial blast furnace here in the wonderful state of Arizona. We chop it up, melt it down, you no worry 'bout what we do. Our concern is yer welfare, our product, and all the fuckin dinero you got in this nice big house. Comprende, amigo?"

"Okay," answered Rory.

***

He was sitting slouched down on the couch in Cuddy's townhouse, the laptop sitting open next to the .38 on the glass coffee table. It was eerily quiet. He had sat on his hams twenty or so minutes after Rory and the big Mexican in black had gone back into the mansion, making sure they weren't tricking him into coming out. When he got back to the townhouse, he parked the Fiat in a parking lot behind the community pool. He didn't want to put it in the carport. He didn't know if he should just jump back in it and take off for home, be done with all of this. Cuddy was dead. Cuddy was *dead*.

This is so fucked up.

Sam wept for a long time, thinking of his lifelong friend, how he was messed up in the head but knew enough to try to get help.

Well, one way to look at it is at least now he isn't suffering. He's with Holly…they're together.

Rachel entered his mind, and he quickly remembered that she was screwing someone else. He felt alone, more than he ever had.

This is so fucked up.

At a moment when he should have been thinking rationally, Sam wanted to do something irrational. He didn't want to just get in the car, drive home, pretend that he didn't know about his wife's affair, that he didn't care about his daughter ignoring him all the time, that he wanted to go back to his boring, pathetic job and life, go on as if Cuddy and Holly had meant nothing to him. Cuddy and Holly were everything to him. Maybe he wasn't in their lives regularly, but he was sure both knew how significant they were. He hoped they had felt the same way about him.

So he reversed roles. What if he were Cuddy, and he just found out that Rory James and his men tossed Sam's dead body into the back of his Fiat. What would Cuddy do?

He'd blow their asses to the moon is what he'd do...because he'd know how to. Cuddy never did care about consequences. He wouldn't have cared about any Mexican drug cartel protecting Rory. He feared no one, save maybe Coach Drago.

Now Holly, Holly was always more sensible...well, before everything.

He felt her presence somehow then, through the heartache and the sorrow.

What do I do here, Holly? Holy shit, what do I do? It falls on me, doesn't it? It falls on me to do the right thing.

He thought of her as a young girl, as a young woman, as a middle-aged stripper, as a junkie dying in a seedy motel with nobody who cared for her but a gang-banging cockroach pimp named Omar.

A gangbanger. Omar. Gangbangin pimp asshole.

He couldn't remember the name of the gang, but so what.

The motel. The Borgata.

Sam sat up, moved to the laptop, and typed in the name. The address came up, Sixteenth and Baseline Road. He sat back again, gently scratching the stubble that had formed on his face, thinking.

It's not impossible. It's dangerous as all hell, but not impossible. It's reckless, but not insane, not completely insane. Offer someone enough praise and money, and they'll do just about any-thing. The two things that everyone wants: praise and money. Gangs like money. Gangs have guns. Gangs have guys who like to shoot guns at other guys.

Remember the upshot. If all goes accordingly, this would be me taking care of everything and everyone...with no consequences.

"It's worth a try," Sam said to himself, leaping up from the couch, grabbing the .38. "What have *I* got to lose?"

24

Gritty Pretty

Outside in the parking lot in front of La Tina Laundromat, Cuddy sat in his open jeep, the blazing heat bearing down on him. He swiped off his shades and cleared his face of a mild sheen of sweat. It was late afternoon, the hottest time of day in the valley, and Cuddy was getting irritated that one of his clients, a local high school football player with a few Division I scholarship opportunities, was late for an exchange.

These young fuckin pizza-face morons can't be trusted. Coach is stupid to be pushing this stuff at this level. These dumb-asses can't even find a fuckin Laundromat, let alone figure out how to inject somatropin.

He sat there watching people shuffling in and out of the place, a small blue soft-sided cooler bag sitting on the floorboard of the passenger seat next to him. An attractive woman carrying a sack of clothes toward the front entrance caught his eye. She was thin and had trouble carrying the large sack, stopping to get a better grip every few steps. She had long raven hair pulled back, numerous tattoos on her arms. A turn-on for Cuddy.

Love that ink, makes them look wild.

She was wearing a thin yellowish summer dress with butterflies on it, a V-neck that complemented ample breasts. The dress stopped at her thighs, long firm but thin legs running down to turquoise leather cowboy boots.

Damn, there's just somethin 'bout a woman in a dress and cowboy boots.

"Now, that's a woman," he said to no one in particular. "Probably about my age and look at her, still rockin it." He watched as she finally hefted the sack of clothes up onto her right shoulder and strolled at a steadier gait. "A real woman. I'd like to…"

She turned her face toward him as she swung the door of the laundry open, sensing the eyes of the handsome muscular guy sitting in the jeep checking her out.

"Holly?" said Cuddy to himself as he watched her disappear into the place.

Just then a silver Dodge Charger roared up and came to an abrupt halt in the parking space next to Cuddy. He tried to peer into the tinted windows but couldn't see a damn thing. He felt the cool waft of air conditioning as a young man lowered the passenger window.

"What's up, Holmes?" said the young man, turning toward Cuddy with a beefy head, stiff jaw, and no neck.

"You're late," snapped Cuddy.

The kid shrugged a massive shoulder. "How do you like my new ride?"

This kid owns a brand-new Dodge Charger?

"Why aren't you driving?"

"Don't have my license yet. This is Collins, he plays for UCLA." The kid gestured toward the driver, a large black man with the same beefy head, hammer jaw, and no neck.

"Yeah, I know Collins. Hey, man. How's the Achilles, C-Train?"

"All fine, thanks to you, brutha," said Collins. "Be back training in no time."

Cuddy looked back at the passenger. "Mommy and Daddy buy you this?"

"Les just say it was an anonymous gift," he replied. "Got my stuff, Holmes?"

Gently, Cuddy reached for the soft-sided cooler and handed it to the passenger in the Charger. "Four-to-six IU per day, two in the morning, two in the—"

"Yeah, I know the fuckin routine, dude," said the kid, shaking his head in annoyance. "What you gonna do next? Remind me that it delivers power, aids recovery, avoids detection, and creates a champion? Shit, man, I already *am* a champion. Go online, check out my highlights, bro."

Cuddy wanted to rip the kid through the window and pound his head against the curb for such lack of respect. "Pay up," he said instead, yet hoping the kid didn't have the payment or only had partial payment, any excuse to beat some manners into the shithead.

This is what you deal with when you deal with kids these days. They walk around with a sense of entitlement. I'll shove entitlement right up his—

The kid leaned out the window and handed Cuddy a grease-stained paper bag from a fast-food restaurant. Cuddy caught the look of the kid's hand and noticed how awkwardly he held the paper bag.

"All of it?" he asked.

When the kid nodded, a wash of disappointment came over Cuddy. "Lower the dosage or pause the cycle for a couple of weeks, dumb-ass," he said, opening his door and stepping out.

"Why's that, Holmes?" barked the kid.

"Cause carpel tunnel is a side effect, and you got it. How do you expect to keep those guys from gettin to your quarterback if your hands are mangled while you're in the trenches?"

"With this…" The kid motioned toward his bulging bicep as Cuddy walked away toward the entrance to the Laundromat. "Just go change your dirty diapers, old-timer."

The Charger roared out of the parking lot.

***

He stood near the door, holding the grease-stained paper bag, just watching her separate her clothes and drop them into a machine. It'd been about a year or so since the last time he had run into her. A tattoo parlor, half her ass exposed, and a grimy bearded guy with a bandana and a leather vest stenciling away.

"Gritty pretty" was the best way to describe her. Guys take one look at her and can't help but wonder what she'd do to them.

As he walked closer, he could make out the dark circles under her eyes, her gaunt facial structure, pale skin.

Damaged, yes, but not broken, still well intact, Holly.

"Would you like me to separate those for you?" He said it suave.

She didn't look up; just smiled. "I thought that was you."

He came up behind her, put his arm around her waist, and kissed her on the cheek. She leaned in to meet the kiss and then spun around and wrapped her arms around him. She kept her head nestled between his shoulder and his neck for a few seconds like a sleeping child. When they separated, they only left a few inches between them.

She looked down at the bag. "You always eat your lunch in a Laundromat parking lot?"

"If there's a chance I might run into a beautiful old friend again, yes."

"Key word there, Jimmer, *old*," she replied. "How you been? You look good."

Cuddy briefly looked down at his pecks and then back up into those blue eyes. "I'm good, same ole same ole, you know." His face turned serious for a moment. "You? You doing all right?"

"Not so bad. Still at the Dream Palace. Good cash, don't have to report it. But this bod isn't what it used to be, so they've been kickin me to waitressing most nights."

"Oh yeah, waitressing?"

"I do miss the dancing, but I've come to find that customers treat the women with clothes on a little better. Besides, the younger girls can do amazing things now."

"Well, you look incredible. Always have, always will."

She smiled again, her teeth too white for her pale skin. Newly whitened or new teeth altogether, Cuddy figured. *She had the money for that.* He glanced at the fleshy part of her forearm for possible needle tracks but didn't see any.

"You always knew how to talk to the girls, Jimmer."

"Cuddy," he corrected her.

She took a half step closer to him now, their faces nearly touching, the other patrons in the Laundromat shooting interested glances their way.

"You'll always be Jimmer to me."

Suddenly, Cuddy felt intoxicated. There was just something about her. Every time he saw her, she put a spell on him. He was sure she wasn't manipulating him. He was hoping she wasn't manipulating him. Not this time. Could she smell the bag of cash? Did she want to go do what they did after they ran into each other at the tattoo parlor or not? Because, of course, he was for sure ready, willing, and able to do that again.

"Where you livin these days?" he asked.

She drew back, hesitating, allowing a little shame to burn through the paleness. "It's temporary until I get a place, but I'm staying at a motel right now, the Borgata, Sixteenth and Baseline Road. Not such a great area, so that's why I'm over here…doing my laundry. Did a load over there once, came back and all my delicates were gone."

"You drive up here or…?"

"Took the bus."

"Well, I'll give you a lift home when your clothes are done."

She smiled again, melting him. "It's good to see you, Jimmer," she said, gently tapping his massive chest.

He caught her quick glance at the fast-food bag, but it didn't change anything. Maybe she was hungry.

"You hungry?"

"Yeah, sure."

"There's a sandwich shop next door. We can grab a bite and wait," he suggested.

"Yeah, let's do that." She took his hand and together they strolled out of the Laundromat like a happy couple.

They spent the hour casually talking about the weather, current events, and the rising prices of everything. A regular ole couple waiting out the rinse cycle. They didn't speak about anything personal, nothing about the past. There were a few awkward silences, but Holly would jump up and go check the laundry. It wasn't long before they were back in the hot sun on their way to her place.

***

Cuddy, in machine-gun-fuck mode, was driving Holly into the motel bed, thrusting and grunting and licking and kissing her tats up and down her breasts. She was holding on for dear life, pretending to enjoy every rigorous stab. She'd fake one absurdly emphatic orgasm. She'd breathlessly stutter his name, "Jim-Jim-Jim-Jim-mer!" She'd ride him like a feral horse, a buckin bronco. She'd go on all fours and let him put it anywhere. She'd go down on him for the finale, just to make him feel good, just to make him feel happy, just to make him feel she appreciated everything he'd done for her and everything he was going to do for her—hopefully do for her.

Gyrating like a hound in heat, he had attempted to look into her eyes, but she either turned away feigning enjoyment or reached down and tickled his balls until his eyes went nearly cross-eyed from the pleasure.

No intimacy here. Work. Just returning a favor. I hope he understands that again.

Exploding like a volcano, muscles flexed to the hilt, face tight and contorted, moan thick, raspy, and drawn-out. He slid out of her mouth and dropped face first onto the mattress, trying to catch his breath. Holly sidled up to him and ran her fingers down the sweat-stained scar on his back.

She paused for a moment, trying to put more time between the end and the inquiry, but felt too compelled.

"You hear from Sam?" she asked and then caught him sighing sullenly.

When he turned over, she rested her head on his chest and began caressing the tattoo on one of his forearms. "It doesn't even look like me," she said softly.

"Just call him, Holly," said Cuddy, raising his head up, smirking at the tat, and then lowering his head back down on the bed. "The guy is miserable. Hearing from you again would make his day, his month, his year, his fuckin miserable life worthwhile."

She was staring off at nothing. "I miss him. I do. I miss everything. You say he's miserable, but he's the one out of us three who has somewhat of a normal life."

"You should have married him when you had the chance."

"You said that the last time we fucked."

His head came up again, "Yeah, well, you bring him up every time we fuck. And you're the one who told me to get this tattoo of you." He raised his forearm and studied the naked woman with the oversized tits and the long jet-black hair riding the motorcycle. "Yer right. It doesn't much look like you."

She lifted herself up and stood at the side of the bed with a portion of the sheet covering her body. Running a hand through her hair she said, "Jimmer, I need some money."

"For what?" He knew, thought he'd ask anyway. See if she'd admit it.

"Pay the rent on this dump. Food. You know…"

"Get high?"

"That, too."

"Where's your track marks?"

"You know"—she shot him an angry look—"it hasn't been easy. I've had to deal with a lot in my life." She seemed on the verge of tears.

"Haven't we all," he replied, lifting a burly arm up and placing it behind his head.

"I need that stuff so I can keep it together."

"That stuff will kill you." He started to get up and put his clothes on.

"I've been taking it for years, Jimmer, and I'm still here. It's my sanctity. It's what keeps me together through all this. I know my limitations. I know the boundaries."

"Holly, do you want me to pay for the sex again, so you can give it to your spic pimp, or do you want me to give you a charitable donation, so you can shoot some heroin into your veins?"

He was standing now, looking at her with an intense glare. "Or maybe you want both."

"Omar takes care of me. If it wasn't for him…I'd probably be dead. And what makes you think you're so different?"

"You're a whore and a junkie," Cuddy snapped.

"If I'm a whore and a junkie, then what does that make you? Look at you. It's not a normal man's body. You do all kinds of drugs, you fuck, god knows, everything with a vagina." She started pointing at him. "Yer a fuckin whore and a junkie! Yer no different than me!"

He stormed toward the door. "Fuck off."

The day's light blinded them both. He stepped out onto the walkway and slammed the door behind him. He could hear her inside call him an asshole.

Down the hall, sitting in plastic chairs in front of one of the rooms, were a few Mexicans, and they all turned his way. One, a short, stocky, bald-headed man with ripped muscles like Cuddy, stood up and walked toward him as he made his way to the stairs that led down to the parking lot. As they passed, the man smiled profoundly, gold teeth caps shimmering in the sunlight.

"Que tenga un buen día," said the Mexican.

"Go tend to your whore, prick," said Cuddy as he went bounding down the stairs.

Sitting on the end of the bed, still holding the sheet around her, Holly looked up. Through her tears, there it was, sitting on the dresser next to the television, the grease-stained paper bag. She rushed over to it, opened it, saw the cash, grabbed a few bills out, and hurriedly shoved the bag into a drawer just as the door opened.

"He pay up, Hail-raizah?"

"Yeah, Omar"—she held up the few bills that she had swiped from the bag—"he paid."

Omar slammed the door, walked over, and grabbed them out of her hand. Then shoved her to the bed and started to unbuckle his belt and shimmy out of his chinos. He always got hard after a John fucked his lady.

Meanwhile, Cuddy fired up the jeep, looked at the tattoo of Holly on his forearm, and…tried desperately not to cry.

25

Omar Rosales

The empty pool, encased by a rusting metal fence, was lit up by the yellow hue of the parking lot lights. From the balcony, Sam could see thick dark muck floating near the drain. A couple of fellows were sitting on a bench on the lower level of the motel, but they weren't really paying him any mind. A couple of the doors on the upper level were open, televisions or music blasting from inside, mixing with the sirens and the cars rushing by outside.

He made his way to one of the rooms where a door was open, knocked on the wood panel, and cautiously stuck his head inside. "Hello?"

There was a skinny black man lying on a bed in sweatpants and a T-shirt. He was eating chicken scraps from what looked to be a trash bag, and he looked up, startled. "You five-O? I done nothin! You five-O?"

"Pardon?"

"Po-leece? Sheeet, you ain't no po-leece."

"No, I'm lookin for Omar. You know which room?"

"Fuck no, I don't know no Omar. Why, whad he do?"

"Nothing. Actually, I'm lookin for…Holly."

"Holly Butane? That's what I called her, cuz man she waz jez so hot, umph! I miss ole Holly Butane. Girl a sparkplug when she wazn't doped up."

Sam nodded.

"She gone, man. Holly Butane done light burned out, 'bout a yea' ago. But now they's Clarista in room twenty-two. She a'right. Little Mexican-Asian girl on da heavy side. An odd breed that one, but I do likes em thataway, on da heavy side. But no ass. Girl got no ass. And flat as a pancake. Got a Mexican ass and Asian tits. Hey, you think you loan me some money?"

Sam stepped back out onto the balcony.

"I could use a few dollah!" He heard the man call out as he walked down to room twenty-two and lightly knocked.

A short, stocky brown-skinned girl with dark narrow eyes and pimples on her face opened the door, revealing only her face and some cleavage.

"You look too old to be one of Mikey's friends. You his daddy or somethin?"

Sam couldn't tell if she was wearing a bikini, or she was in her underwear or nothing at all. She kept the door open just enough for a tease. He didn't know how to answer the question either, so he stood there.

"You a cop?"

"No—"

"Two hundred straight, three up the ass—No, since I don't know you, cowboy, three hundred straight and four up the ass. Show me the cash first."

"I'm a friend of Holly's."

The girl broke character, her assertive expression dropping from her face. Suddenly she looked ten years younger, maybe even a teenager. "Hold on," she said and closed the door. She opened it seconds later wearing a long peach-colored camisole and told him to come in. She went right to the bed, sat down, lit a cigarette, and leaned back against the headboard, not worrying whether the camisole was covering anything or not.

The room held a rancid odor. Sam entered but kept the door open.

"I miss Holly," said the girl. "She was good people. You want me to pretend to be her, do the things she did to ya? Well, cowboy, I ain't exactly got her chest if you know what I mean, but…" she chuckled.

Sam wanted to tell her to shut the fuck up and let him do the talking, but he figured it would probably be wise to approach this delicately. Maybe he wouldn't have to close the door and pull the .38.

"Wasn't anything like that. I grew up with Holly. I was hoping you knew where I could find her boyfriend."

The girl finished her drag and scrunched up her face as if she had no idea what he was talking about. "Boyfriend?" she exhaled the smoke, "There ain't no boyfriends in this business."

"Omar."

She squinted, lifted a knee, and rested her arm on it, while ash from the cigarette fell to the carpet. "What you want with Omar?"

Sam didn't bother to look between her legs. "What do you think I want with him?"

That was a gamble, but if that doesn't do it, I'm gonna need to do something drastic.

"Omar one bad muthafucker, cowboy. Him not comin round here no more would sure help me save some money. But he fuck you up, then you ain't never met me. No, you never here."

Sam nodded, and looked down between her legs. The girl flashed a winning smile. "He's gotta crib on the eastside, 1001 Cocopah Avenue, but they all gangbangers down there, cowboy. Got homies all over the place, and he don't like strangers, especially white dudes."

"Thanks, Clarista."

"My name ain't Clarista"—her leg went down—"It's Maria."

Another lost soul. Maybe she had something tragic happen to her at a young age. A father, a stepfather? Some sick bastard turned her into this.

He headed for the doorway, but before stepping out, he turned back and fetched a few twenties from his wallet. He put the money on the end of the bed. It felt familiar. A few years back he had done the same for Holly.

"I'll suck it for fifty, cowboy."

"Thanks, Maria," he said and walked out.

***

After a slow and cautious drive-by on Cocopah Avenue, Sam parked the Fiat a few blocks away next to a sign that read WARNING: This area protected by Neighborhood Watch. Suspicious Activity Call Crime Stop…and then it listed a number. He wondered if the sign did anything to prevent crime or bad elements in this neighborhood. He tucked the .38 into the glove compartment, got out, and headed down the street. It was late now, nearing midnight, but there was steady movement in the faint darkness outside the glow of distant streetlights. Here and there were young men, mostly in hoodies and oversized pants, standing on corners, sitting on porches, mumbling to one another, ambling around with no real destination.

It was a small brown brick ranch home, didn't look too imposing.

It didn't have the look of a gangbanger's residence, whatever that look was.

The place had a screen on the front door, a carport with a white El Camino and a motorcycle parked inside. There was no one out front when he drove by.

As he approached the block, he noticed the overgrown vegetation, the gravel driveways, and the beaten-up mailboxes on crooked posts. He walked on the street, because there were no sidewalks. A few houses down, he had passed a group of men huddled in a carport, hoodies on, speaking Spanish to one another. They looked to be drinking forties from brown paper bags. They seemed to all look up at once.

Sam veered to the other side of the street and was about to walk through the yard of the brown brick home toward the front door when someone called out, "Where the fuck you think yer goin?"

He turned and saw a man heading toward him at a fast gait. "I'm lookin for O—"

His jaw vibrated, and he fell back, knocking over a mailbox and its wobbly post. His shoes kicked at the gravel as he hurriedly crawled on his back and elbows, reaching the curb, seeing the man ripping off the hoodie and bearing down on him.

"Who you with?" yelled the man. "You don't come in Milpas country without permission!"

"Fuck, no one! I'm not with…"

The kick landed in his lower gut, but the jolt of pain still sucked the air from his lungs. The hard sole of someone's boot landed on the side of his head and stayed there, pressing the right side of his face into the cement. Suddenly, he felt the same dull pressure on both forearms. From the corner of his left eye he could make out the end of a barrel pointed at his face. As the barrel teetered from side to side, he could see two men standing directly over him, both Mexican. One had a foot on his head and right forearm, the other stood on his left forearm and pointed a handgun sideways at his face. He wondered if they were going to blow the right side of his face off just for walking down a street at midnight.

"Talk before I turn yer head into a busted piñata!"

Lungs still on fire, Sam couldn't get the words out.

"You here to score smack? You buy that shit between Seventh and Sixteenth! Who told you to come in here?"

"No…no one. I'm lookin for Omar."

"Whatya want with Omar?"

"Business."

The man pumped the shotgun and pressed it against Sam's temple.

Spitting and stuttering, Sam managed, "Business, a business propo-proposition. A lot of fuckin cash. I have a lot of fuckin cash. I want him—I need him—to help me with something."

The barrel of the shotgun came off his temple, as did the pressure on his head and arms. He heard the man carrying the shotgun with one hand, like a long pistol, say, "Get him up and bring him in back."

He was lifted by several men and dragged through the carport, through the doorway of an open fence where two pit bulls attached to chain leashes barked and snapped at him as he went by. He was dropped on the ground in front of a small patio. The man with the shotgun was sitting at a table, the gun resting on it. He told someone to shut the dogs up and another to search the man on the ground for any weapons.

That's when Sam realized there were at least a half dozen of them all either holding a handgun or with one stuck in their waistbands, all with flannel shirts on buttoned only at the neck, and either baggy jeans or oversized chinos, all bald, all short and stocky.

"Fuck that, check him for a wire, too!" said the man sitting at the table. "They could have drones up there." He pointed up into the night's sky.

After they were done patting and prodding, Sam finally got a glimpse of the man at the table. His was evil-looking—scars, wrinkles, burns, deep divots in his face, a dark goatee that had hints of gray in it, a domed-shaped bald head, and dark-set eyes. He seemed to have an expression that looked like he was always scowling or in excruciating pain. And the shotgun barrel wasn't as long as Sam thought. It was sawed off, and the gun had a pistol handle.

Maybe this wasn't such a good idea.

"What you doin in my 'hood, boy?"

Sam sat up, brushing himself off and gently touching the cut on his lower lip from the blow to his jaw. He could taste the blood in his mouth. "I've got a business proposition."

"A business what, muthafucka?"

"A…an opportunity for you, your guys, your gang, to make some money."

"Who the fuck are you?"

"I ain't talkin to anyone unless it's Omar."

"You ain't what? Fuck you! I tell you what you gonna do and what you not gonna do!"

And with those words Sam noticed the gap in the man's mouth.

Yep, his two front teeth were gone. Omar. Cuddy really did knock his teeth out.

"Listen, there's a guy I know who sells a lot of drugs, sort of a major player in the high end of drug trafficking. He lives in a mansion up north on the side of a mountain. He's got a shitload of cash in that mansion, a shitload, untraceable cash, just sitting there waiting for someone to take it."

"Who is this guy you know?"

"His name is Rory James. He played minor league baseball years ago, decades ago."

"And how you know him?"

Sam paused and looked around. The six others were staring intently at him. "We grew up together."

"What you want—us to steal the money and give you a cut?"

"No, I don't want any of the money. I just think the guy is an asshole, and I'd like to see him get burned is all."

"That's it?"

"That's all."

"How come you not steal the money, piss off yer friend?"

"He's not my friend," Sam replied sternly. "And I think it's pretty obvious I'm not cut out for…that kind of thing. You and your men here are, I assume, professionals. I mean the … the Milpas are well-known."

"Well-known," the man beamed proudly.

"Yeah. You guys are the meanest, the most ruthless, the toughest gang in all of Phoenix. That's one of the reasons I came here."

"Tell me about this guy with all this money."

"He's got a few guys who work for him that may put up a little fight."

"What kind of guys?"

Sam looked around. "Mexicans."

"A gang?"

"No, just guys who work for him."

"How many guys?"

"Just a few."

"They carry guns?"

"No. Well, yeah, probably. Maybe two or three of the guys. But this guy isn't in a gang or anything, and he isn't a badass. It'd be an easy…uh, an easy score. He's got loads of cash just layin round."

The man snapped up and grabbed the handle of the shotgun. He lowered the weapon at Sam. "Now for the most important question! Why did you come down my street and try to walk up on my crib?"

The fear was real, but Sam felt himself acting.

"Like I said the Milpas are badass mutherfuckers." Right away he could tell this guy needed more. "And Holly, my friend Holly, told me about Omar a while back. Said he was the best of the gangbangers, the baddest of the bad, said he was invincible. You're Omar, right?"

Omar sat back and rested the shotgun across his lap. "Shame what happened to that bitch. Girl had a smokin hot body, even as old as she was. Some of these niños pequeños wanted to fuck her," he pointed toward the other men, "made them pay, too!" He guffawed, revealing more of the gap and the twisted mess of teeth in his mouth. Some of the men grinned and grunted. He settled again and looked seriously at this white boy on the ground in front of him. He could kill him, have the boys bury him somewhere out in the desert. He could beat him down a little more and tell him to never come back to this neighborhood again. Or he could trust him and hopefully make a big, much-needed score for himself and, well, maybe the Milpas—and then kill him and have the boys bury him somewhere out in the desert.

The fact was, things were getting thin for Omar Rosales and his crew, and for the entire Las Cuatro Milpas. The drug market had grown stale and the Maricopa County Sheriff's Department was cracking down on everyone and everything gang related. Something called a civil injunction where you were sent up for just being associated with a gang was wreaking havoc on recruiting. Durango, Tent City and Towers jails had been filling up with not only Milpas but numerous members from rival gangs. Omar's fourth cousin, Chiquito, with a rap sheet full of petty misdemeanors, was slapped with a civil injunction and two weeks later arrested when he stopped by Omar's house to drop off a new fan belt for the El Camino.

Omar was working part time at Home Depot for extra money and skimming what he could from the hookers in his circle. Even that was getting to be a pain in the ass. More and more the girls were becoming defiant, standing up for themselves, even demanding no freebies.

Home Fuckin Depot, man!

In that little orange vest, helping annoying rich couples pick out tile for their bathrooms. He was sick of this straight-line bullshit. Took him a few weeks to make enough money to buy new chrome rims for the Camino.

Suckers were two hundred apiece!

And he had given up on getting those gold teeth replaced.

Fifteen to twenty-five hundred! I kill that muthafucka, I ever come across him again!

The long sharp knife came out of a sheath from behind his back. "You fuckin with me, I will gut you."

Sam nodded, as if that sounded reasonable.

"How much cash we talkin here?" asked Omar. "Wait." He gestured toward the other men. "Y'all go on back over to Chente's crib. I got this now. Take Bruno and Pug with ya, I'm tired of them rug rats shittin and pissin in my momma's yard."

The men filed out, the dogs leading one of them.

"I can't give an exact amount on it, but I imagine it's probably in the hundred-thousand-dollar range at least," said Sam. He couldn't determine if Omar thought the amount too low or not. The man just sat there, that steely, angry look on his face. "But along with that, there's likely plenty of drugs, and whatever else you want in the mansion is yours to take. I really don't care."

"You must really hate this muthafucka."

"Yeah, I do." Sam motioned if he could sit on the chair across from Omar at the table. Omar nodded. "That's why I've got just one request in all this."

"Oh now, see, here it comes. I knew there be somethin." He was still holding the blade and pointed it at this dipshit who'd walked into his life tonight. "Think real hard before you go makin any fucked-up requests."

"I just want him kept alive. I don't want you or your guys killing him."

"Why's that? You hate the muthafucka so much, you shouldn't care if he takes one in the head." Omar drew forward and leaned his upper body on the table. His face was even more menacing close up. "We don't want no one who can ID us."

"I want to kill him," said Sam.

It took Omar a good full minute to let that sink in, but now he was convinced, convinced beyond a doubt. "You gonna kill him with me watchin," he replied, nodding and pointing the blade. "See, that's how that's gonna go down. Comprende?"

"When can you do it?"

Omar could sense the urgency in this guy's hard stare. "You wanna go tonight, don't you, white boy? Let me ask you something. Holly seemed to know a big muscled-up muthafucka that used to come around a bit. I sliced him open the day she OD'd. You know where I could find that muthafucka? Like to finish the job."

"Didn't know her that well." There was a long silence, and Sam didn't take his eyes off Omar. They seemed to be in a stare down.

Omar broke first. "Well, why not?" He sheathed the knife. "We got nothin better to do tonight." He stood up. "Two of my homies ride with you. You try anything, they'll cut yer throat and leave you by the side of the road. Rest of my vatos goin with me in the Camino. Just as soon as we lock and load.

"Chente!" Omar hollered, and a minute later a man came running through the gate and into the yard. "We goin on this job. Bring over the Mac 90s, and have the boys pack Glocks with the extended clips. Everyone loaded."

Chente hurried out the gate.

"How'd you know I had a car?" asked Sam.

"That little gay red ride you floated in on? We got spotters in this 'hood everywhere—mothers, grandmothers, brothers, cousins, uncles, aunts. Got about twenty pings you were on yer way in. Oh, that reminds me, you gonna fix my mailbox, muthafucka."

26

It's Her Life

She told him on a Tuesday morning, before school. They were in the parking lot. It was the first thing she had said to him in weeks, even though he tried calling, tried stopping by her house, tried to chat with her at school. He didn't see her walk up. She seemed to appear from nowhere. He got out of his little old two-door Honda Civic, grabbed his books, and was headed to the locker area when there she was, standing between two cars, holding her books to her chest, her long dark hair falling over her face. She barely looked up.

"I'm pregnant."

***

It ruined Sam's day. He had exams, but he couldn't focus on anything else. He hadn't been able to focus on anything at all for a while. Too distracted. Later that day, he sat in the cafeteria and stared at Rory James, his muscular physique, his fancy clothes. He watched him smirk, while someone nearby went on about another phenomenally pitched game. The hatred boiled up, and the frustration was overpowering. Weeks of seeing him going on about his business like nothing so despicable had ever been done. No more.

Sam stood up and gaited down the line of tables. When he reached Rory he unleashed a wild roundhouse, but Rory had seen him coming and expected it. He ducked and popped Sam straight in the nose. The group around Rory laughed and went about their high-fiving as Sam fell to the ground in between the tables.

"What the fuck is your problem, McElroy?" someone squawked.

***

"What happened?" asked the nurse, grabbing a white towel off a counter and pressing it against Sam's face.

"My nose started bleeding," he answered.

"Well, they're prone to do that in dry weather. Pinch it and then clean yourself off, and it's back to class, mister. Your future depends on it." She went to attend to a freshman tossing his lungs out in a trash can in another room.

Sam sat there, his nose throbbing, his eyes glassy.

I don't know how she can go to class. I don't know how she can walk past him. I don't know how she can function. I'm in awe of her. I'm disappointed in her. Why won't she go to the police?

He stood up, put the towel under some running water, and in the mirror damped the blood on his face. Looking out the hall and straight across into the administration office, he noticed the principal talking to someone, possibly a teacher who might have seen the pathetic fight in the cafeteria. He could go right in there and tell her everything, and it would be over. The cops would be here, and they'd cuff Rory James and toss him into the back of a cop car.

But Jimmer's words kept creeping into his mind. "It's her life. It's her decision. You don't get to decide what she wants to do. This happened to her, not you, not me. To her. It's her life."

It's her life. It's her life. It's her life.

He finished washing the dried blood off his face and left the nurse's office. Holly was leaving a class when he stopped her and told her he needed to talk.

"What happened to your face?" she asked, but he ignored the question.

They ended up in his car and then in the parking lot of a fast-food restaurant. He took her hand. "I'll do anything you want, Holly."

"Well, I'm not keeping it, Sam," she said matter-of-factly, before the tears started to slip down her cheeks. She moved her head about as if she were fighting the urge to cry or tired of crying. "I'm a teenager. I was raped, and I never went to the police. I can't go to my parents and suddenly say I'm pregnant and...Gawd, they'd freak out about that alone...they'd really go bonkers over the other. And then what do I do? I'm eighteen, and I have a baby to care for from someone who's a monster." She looked at Sam, her face in shambles. "I can't have a baby, Sam. I am a baby."

He put his arm around her and pulled her into his chest as she cried heavier.

"I wasn't going to tell anyone," she said.

"Like an—an abortion? I mean, I don't know the law," he asked. "Can you?"

"Yeah, eighteen. I don't need anyone's consent. I've already talked to a doctor at a clinic and set up an appointment. I'll need you to drive me home." She looked up at him. She shook her head when she said it, as if the burden she felt was sitting there in the car with them. "I'm sorry, Sam."

"Why do you keep apologizing to me? I'll drive you there and wait with you, and I'll drive you home. I told you, I'll do anything you want me to do."

Strong words, but she could sense the slight apprehension in his voice. "Please don't think I'm doing the wrong thing," she said. "I need you to understand. I really do. I can get through all this with your support. I know I can, Sam."

"I'm with you, Holly. I support you. Tell the cops, don't tell the cops. Have it, don't have it. Whatever you want to do. It's your life, not mine."

***

Lying awake that night, he realized how coarse he'd sounded in the car.

That's no way to support someone. You want to make the wrong decision, well then, I support you, because you're the one making the wrong decision, not me. Fuckin idiot. Holly doesn't deserve this, no one deserves this. She's an incredible girl, full of love and life, and love of life. She's being shattered by all this. Maybe I can change it. Maybe I owe her that, anyway.

He was waiting outside her house in the morning, his car running at the curb. Her mother looked at him oddly. "Yes, Sam?"

"If you don't mind, Mrs. Karlan, I'd like to drive Holly to school."

Mrs. Karlan turned around and looked at Holly, her head lowered, and her eyes looking at the ground. She nodded approval and trotted off to Sam's car.

"Holly, promise me you'll do something with your *hair* before you get to school. You look like you haven't brushed it in weeks!" hollered Mrs. Karlan.

On a backstreet near school, he pulled over to the side of the road. "I know what we can do…I know what we can do to make this thing somehow work out."

"Sam, I'm not—"

"I love you, Holly. I've loved you forever. I think I first knew it when you took my hand at that holiday recital when we were in like first grade, and we were singing those songs in front of everyone with our class. You remember? Jimmer kept teasing us and messing up the words?" She smiled and wiped her eyes, holding back more tears that were sure to flow. "I'll always love you," he continued, fidgeting in the seat. "We say I got you pregnant. You keep it. I'll go to school here somewhere instead of the Midwest. We raise it. Down the road, we get married. You—*we*—put all this behind us."

Holly's waterfall of tears followed a deep sigh.

"I love you, too, Sam, and now I think you're even more incredible than I already thought you were. But one ruined life is enough. I'm not going to do that." She held up her hand trying desperately to speak through the emotion. "I won't let that happen. I won't allow what he did, what happened, to unsettle more lives. I won't. I appreciate it, and I love you so much, too, and I always will, but I'll take care of this on my own, and I'll get on with my life, and I'll be fine. I'll be just fine. Everything will work out, you'll see. And you and me, we'll see each other someday when we're older, and we'll be so proud of who we are and what we've become. We'll be living happy lives, and maybe, maybe we'll be together."

***

It was storming heavily on the day of the appointment. Sam shielded her from the rain with his windbreaker as they hurried up the ramp to the small clinic. There was some idle chitchat with a nurse and the doctor about the weather before the doctor got serious about the procedure, something about a suction curette and a cannula tube, and off Holly went to a back room.

"It will only take about fifteen minutes, and then I'll let you back there," the nurse, an older, bespectacled lady with short and thin red hair, said to Sam. "We'll need to keep her here for observation for a couple of hours, but then it will be okay to take her home."

Sam nodded. "Thank you."

"You two are a cute couple," she replied.

*Fifteen minutes can seem like a lifetime when you're waiting for...*They're running, the three of them, running and skipping down the street. Balloons, bicycles, popsicles. They are jumping on the trampoline in her backyard, trying to climb the tree on the corner near Jimmer's house, swimming in the pools, watching movies, laughing so hard they can't breathe. Singing songs, playing school, arguing over stupid stuff. Grade school, middle school, high school. That first dance. That first kiss.

Stealing golf balls off the fairways of the golf courses. They're listening to music, hard rock music, heavy metal music, the bands with long hair and makeup. Drummer has one arm now, man! Jimmer, you got a mullet! Sammy Mac, you got a crop and a tail! Cool! Their fists in the air and rockin out. Hangin out in Sam's room, the three of them, just talkin, talkin about anything and everything. Holly calling it a day, going home for dinner. Jimmer hardly ever going home, crashing out on a chair in the room.

We'll be going our separate ways soon, well, sort of. I'll be leaving at least.

Sam pondered that thought for a moment.

They won't have that nucleus, the center anymore. Holly at Arizona State, joining a sorority no doubt, and god knows what Jimmer will do, will be, just talks about how Coach Drago is turning him into a muscle machine. Guy has been working out like a fiend the last few weeks. Think he said somethin 'bout taking law enforcement courses at Scottsdale Community College or somethin. Maybe I should be workin out. I wonder what the girls are like in the Midwest—

Just like that, the nurse appeared again. "I can take you back now. Everything went swell."

"You okay?" he asked, taking Holly's hand. He noticed right off, her face was a milky pale.

"Yeah, just feel a little uncomfortable and tired, a little nauseated."

The doctor whipped into the space by a flip of the curtain that separated other lounge chairs in the room. He was tall and bald and spoke in a serious tone.

"Okay, you'll begin feeling better gradually as the sedative wears off. Most women can go back to their daily routines by the next day, but avoid strenuous activity for a few days to prevent unnecessary pain or bleeding. Most women experience some spotting or bleeding. It may last only a few days or as long as two weeks." He cleared his throat. "To prevent infection we advise not to put anything in the vagina—tampons, sex, douching, that sort of thing—for two weeks. We're available twenty-four hours a day for urgent medical calls. You can always reach us with a routine question or concern during normal office hours. Any questions or concerns at this time?"

Holly shook her head. The doctor looked at Sam and nodded, then back at Holly. "Okay then, the nurse will let you know when you can leave. Have a nice day."

Holly said thank you to the curtain, because the doctor had already vanished behind it.

Sam interrupted a lengthy, awkward silence. "Why don't you try to take a little nap."

She looked at him intently, and managed a tight-lipped smile. "Okay. And…thanks, Sam."

He sat down in a chair and began to thumb through a magazine, but her gaze was powerful, so he looked up. He drew the same tight-lipped smile and went back to the magazine. When he looked up again, she still had her blue eyes upon him. He thought maybe he should lighten the mood a little bit. There was always Jimmer to lighten moods, but he wasn't here.

"Hey, you know what Jimmer's up to these days? He's working out like crazy. Coach Drago, the football coach, is training him or something. Every day after school he's in the weight room pumping iron. It's crazy. I've hardly talked to him in weeks."

"Yeah? Good for Jimmer," said Holly.

"Oh shit, that reminds me. The last time I talked to him, he told me to start referring to him as just Cuddy or J. Cuddy. No more Jimmer. Said that's what Drago calls him, Cuddy, and he likes it."

"Little Jimmer Cuddy's growin up." Holly's statement started out strong and then drifted away.

"He's a nut." Sam looked up to see Holly maybe snicker, but her eyes were closed, and she was breathing peacefully. She was asleep.

27

Trembling Hands

There were no homes, no mansions to speak of for miles in this section of mountain. *Except for one,* thought Sam, *and that was a good thing, considering what was about to go down.*

After passing the long stone driveway, the main road eventually turned to dirt and came to an end at a flat area. That's where Sam steered the Fiat, the lights off, two of Omar's men in the car with him keeping quiet, looking around, guns at the ready. He coasted to the place where he had parked the car several hours before. The El Camino followed with two men in the cab—Omar driving—and two sitting in the back, two Mac 90 assault rifles and the sawed-off shotgun with the pistol handle wrapped in a blanket between them.

On the way up to this job that had fallen into his lap, Omar had told the man in the cab of the Camino, his cousin Chente, that they would waste the white boy after they had the money. "I'll let him do what he wants to do to this guy"—Omar had chuckled—"but he ain't leavin alive. That way it's the perfect score, primo!"

Chente had replied enthusiastically, "Sí, ese, ain't nobody know we do this."

Sam had made some suggestions on how to approach the mansion: climb up a rocky slope as he had done earlier and then look down on the house before closing in on it. "Perhaps you go in from the backyard?"

Omar had only grinned enough to show that dark gap and those twisted and crumpled teeth around it. He ordered one of his guys to stay with Sam. The guy, short and portly, scowled at Omar. "Ah c'mon, homey. I wanna bust a cap in some white rich mofos!" But Omar stopped grinning, and his face went back to that evil expression.

Sam reminded Omar that he wanted Rory James alive. When Omar asked what he looked like, Sam had responded, "You'll know which one he is."

They had pulled the guns from the back of the El Camino and checked them. Omar put a Glock in his waistband and picked up the shotgun. He had then ordered everyone into the El Camino, and they took off back down the dirt road, the brake lights eventually lighting up, and the car making a sharp left turn and heading up the driveway toward the mansion.

Gunfire soon erupted. It echoed off the mountain and the rocks. Sam and the guard couldn't see what was happening, but they could hear it. Staccato gunfire, crisp, sharp cracks in the night, growing more intense with every second. Sam walked over to the passenger door that the guard had left open. He looked out at the valley, wondering if anyone could hear the gunfire. The guard had taken a few steps down the road, looking concerned, listening intently, gripping his Glock. "I no like this, homey. I the best shot in the Milpas. Nobody shoot like me. I good," he mumbled.

Automatic rifle fire continued, followed by multiple short pops from a handgun, followed by multiple blasts from a shotgun, followed by more automatic rifle fire.

A scream rang out, and the guard nervously swung around and pointed his Glock at Sam, who slowly put his hands up. The guard then lowered the gun and turned back around, fidgeting. After another scream from the direction of the mansion, he spun around again and told Sam to throw him the keys to his piece-of-shit car. He tucked them into his pocket. "Stay the fuck here!" he said and wobbled down the road on foot.

Sam popped the glove compartment open and grabbed the .38. He made a beeline up the rocky slope, dodging the shadowy outlines of boulders and chollas, thanks to a brilliant moon overhead. When he reached the top, he looked down and saw the guy who was supposed to stay with him jogging up the driveway and into the house. The gunfire continued to roar. As he made his way through the scrub and over a ledge of shale that led down to the expansive backyard, Sam could also hear glass shattering, muffled moans, and the dull thud of drywall exploding.

By the time he made it into the backyard, the gunfire had lessened considerably, drawing down to only the occasional pop-pop.

"Chente! Chente! Oh fuck, primo!" It was Omar's voice, and it was followed by a shotgun blast.

Sam carefully stepped through a shattered sliding door and into a dark room. A spider web of cracks ran through an enormous flat screen television on one wall. On another wall an enormous framed portrait of Rory James standing on a pitcher's mound was hanging over a marble fireplace, untouched by any wayward bullets. On the floor, lined up, were duffel bags brimming with bundles of cash.

As he made his way out into a hallway, the view of the foyer opened up. Bloody bodies were strewn everywhere across the tile floor, including the plump man who, only minutes ago, had left him at his car. He had been shot through the face. Pools of blood were forming from each lifeless body.

"Get back in yer room!" It came from up above. "Boss, I sorry, but this shit is real!"

"I kill you, muthafucka!" It emanated from farther down the hall to Sam's right, and it was quickly followed by another shotgun blast, which was quickly answered by sporadic pops from an assault rifle.

He saw the cowboy boots first as a man stumbled out of a room and into the hall, leaning against a wall and holding an assault rifle with one hand. It was the big Mexican man in black, and he raised his head up. "Gringo!" he screamed. He let burst two pot shots down the hall and stumbled forward, dragging one of his legs. "Gringo!"

"I'll come get you when this over," he heard someone upstairs bellow.

Rory must be upstairs, thought Sam.

The same man from above answered, "Up here!"

Sam dipped back into the entrance of the dark room and squeezed into a corner.

"They's no more comin through the door," hollered the man from above.

"Get yer gringo ass down here and help me with this fucker with the shotgun!"

Just then, all one sound: A pump-click, a blast, a groan, a splatter, and then a thud.

"You killed me cousin, bitch!"

Another pump-click, another blast, another splatter, but no thud. Omar let out an enormous roar. Sam lowered himself to his haunches to stay out of sight. *Why did I come into the fuckin house?*

He was going to bolt back out the shattered sliding door and up the rock slope and wait for whatever was to come, but...someone was on his way down from upstairs, someone who wasted the guys in the foyer. *The guys in the foyer!* Sam remembered his keys. In the pocket of the plump guy lying in a pool of blood.

***

It was only a matter of chance that Cortez peered into the little closet near the front door. The men were partying in the game room, drinking, smoking cigars, and watching a soccer match via satellite. Cortez was still spooked by the incident the night before when two of his men were killed, shot by some guy his boss said he knew during high school or something. The guys from Caborca didn't seem distressed at all that earlier in the evening they had removed and disposed of three bodies and a jeep. It was nothing to them. They were in the game room hooting and hollering about a damn soccer match.

Before sticking his head in to glance at the monitors, Cortez had stopped and inspected the door of the closet.

Looking through the bullet holes, he felt a twinge of fear in his chest. The Bushmaster was resting against a wall in the closet. Seeing it seemed to put him at ease again. Standing next to it was one of the M27s, and that made him feel a whole lot better. But when he glanced at the monitors he had to do a double take.

A fuckin white El Camino, men, machine guns.

"We got more company! They got guns!"

He swiped up the M27 and hurried up the stairs. At the top he popped in a clip and aimed the rifle at the front door. Rory James came out of his room wearing his black robe and holding a Glock. "Go back, boss. They heavily armed!" Rory did what he was told, cinching up his robe and scurrying back into the master suite.

These guys aren't gonna bother ringin the doorbell. They won't be smilin like that big dude with his camouflage rifle before he blew Hosk's face off.

At the first blast the oak door splintered near the handle. A second blast flung it open, and in came a swarm of men with guns.

Cortez picked off the first man through the door, which was a good thing, because he was carrying a large assault rifle. But then two more popped through, and a line of bullets ripped open the wall behind him. As he fired wildly, Cortez noticed a man stroll through the door as if he owned the mansion, holding a pistol-handled sawed-off shotgun at his side. The man pointed at Cortez and said something to one of the other men, then stepped over the sprawled-out dead man and moved into the home, raising the shotgun. Another man followed him in, staying close behind. Cortez missed both, because the spindles of the railing in front of him were blasting apart and spraying wood splinters into his face.

One man began to make his way up the steps while shooting. Cortez dropped lower to the floor, drew a bead on the man's legs and squeezed off a burst from the M27. Most of the bullets ripped through more spindles farther down the stairs and slipped between the man's strides, but one caught a portion of his left shin. The man screamed out in agony.

Two other men came through the door and began firing up at Cortez. He quickly retreated by crawling back behind a wall. When he turned to look down the hall, he saw his boss standing at the entrance to the master suite, Glocks in both hands. Rory James was edging his way toward the stairs hesitantly.

He looks pathetic, thought Cortez, *like he wants to take a heroic stand, perhaps Scarface-style, but just doesn't have the courage or maybe the cocaine to go through with it. Why should I die for this man?*

"Give me the M27, Hermie!"

As the corner of the wall exploded with bullets, Cortez roused, stood up, and emerged from cover. He began firing valiantly—the rifle booming with life. First he went at the man on the steps, then he swung to the other two men down in the foyer, closing his eyes as bullets zipped past his head, his ears, and between his legs. Then the gun went silent, the trigger unresponsive. The rank smell of gunpowder caused him to open his eyes. It was quiet. The man on the stairs was face down, blood oozing from his head. The two men below were torn to pieces, one bleeding mostly from the neck, the other from the abdomen. Cortez stood momentarily impressed and surprised by his work.

And then Rory James came running past him. He watched as his boss raised both hands and began firing the two Glocks down into the foyer, hitting nothing but drywall and floor tile until a short and heavy man stepped through the doorway and into one of the bullets with his face. He fell instantly.

Cortez and Rory stood staring at the bloody corpses below. Finally, Cortez snapped out of the shock and turned to his boss. "Get back in yer room!" He switched out a clip and glared at Rory. "Boss, I sorry, but this shit is real!"

Forlornly, Rory James began to retreat back to the room, his robe billowing out again behind him.

Someone from below began screaming about their cousin. "I kill you, muthafucka!" A blast from a shotgun followed, and then successive pops from a rifle. Rory stopped and turned around. Cortez could see the fear return in his eyes.

"Gringo!" It was Renato Velasquez's deep voice, but it sounded anxious. Two shots cut through the air somewhere down there. "Gringo!"

Cortez said to Rory, "I'll come get you when this over." He turned back in the direction of the foyer. "Up here! They's no more comin through the door."

"Get yer gringo ass down here and help me with this fucker with the shotgun!"

Slowly, Cortez began to make his way down the stairs. He got as far as the fourth step from the top when a shotgun went off again. It sounded like someone took the round directly.

"You killed me cousin, bitch!"

Another shotgun blast rang out and then someone roared like a triumphant lion that had just pounced on its prey. Renato Velasquez was dead, Cortez knew. Which meant his men were likely already dead as well.

Who in the hell is gonna clean this mess up?

He continued to move slowly down the stairs, passing the bullet holes in the wall from where T-Ray had nearly shot the man from the night before.

What the fuck had gone wrong? Everything was going good for us.

Carefully, he made his way around the dead body lying face down and then the bodies and the pools of blood in the foyer. He kept the M27 trained on the hallway leading to the game room. There was no one there except the bloody corpse of Velasquez, his body resting on its side below a splatter of blood that spread across the wall of the hallway.

Two shots from a handgun rang out, and Cortez felt a shove to his left shoulder and ribcage. He stumbled back. The internal burning began. He looked down to see blood streaming from two holes in his shirt. When he looked back up again a stocky bald Mexican was pointing a Glock point-blank at his head. The man grinned, revealing a toothless gap in his mouth. It was the last thing Cortez saw before he died.

***

Wielding both a Glock and the sawed-off shotgun, Omar paced about the main floor of the mansion, mumbling, "Oh, Chente. Mi primo. Mi hombres! Fuck, man! Oh, Chente."

Sam remained hunched in the corner shadow of the living room, the .38 in his trembling hands. Omar entered the room and turned on the lights. Before he could mumble another word, his grief was overcome with bliss.

"Holy shhhit!"

He stood staring at the duffel bags full of cash. Smiling like it hurt, that gap, those snarled teeth exposed,

Omar walked over to the money, dropped his weapons, picked up a few bundles of cash and rubbed them against his chest, moaning and groaning as if he were pleasuring himself.

"Omar is *king*! Omar is *rich*!" He exclaimed.

Trembling hands and all, the bullet from the .38 hit its mark square in the back of Omar's head. He fell face first onto the cash.

"Omar is *dead*," said Sam, his hands still trembling. *For Cuddy and for Holly.*

He took a deep breath and made his way through the foyer and up the stairs, pointing the .38 out before him, a man on a mission, a man who had been waiting for what was to come for twenty-five years.

28

Unscathed

Never in a million years did I picture it going down like it did. Maybe I'd be digging a hole in a desert somewhere, and I'd drag his pathetic ass over to it and dump him in and then just start shoveling the dirt on top of him until he was covered up. Bury him alive, make him suffer a little bit until the end came and he was sent to the fiery bowels of hell.

Why should it be quick and easy for him? Holly was tormented a lifetime for what he did. Why should his end be quick and painless?

The fact is, Rory James suffered a great deal. I found him in a secret room off a walk-in closet of the master bedroom. It was full of all sorts of nasty sexual shit. He came out firing guns like a madman, but when he ran out of bullets, I was still standing there unscathed.

Act of God or just fate? I don't know.

Yes, Rory James suffered a great deal. The best part about it was he *remembered* me. As he lay there writhing in pain, I told him, all this, all of it was for what he did that night to Holly Karlan. I said, "You had this comin to you for a long time. I just wish I had done something sooner."

What made it easier was that he said he didn't remember any Holly Karlan.

Sure, he begged and pleaded, offered me a fortune. But what he didn't realize is that he had already taken everything I ever wanted. He had taken my friends and my life. He had taken my soul.

The cops would find him in that secret room among all that weird kinky shit, packets of his own drug shoved down his throat—I found some on a nightstand next to the bed—his eyes swollen shut, his nose smashed into a portion of his brain, most of his teeth knocked out, his manhood blown from his body, a bullet hole in a thigh, in an armpit, in a kneecap, bleeding profusely, barely breathing. They would find him alive. They would assume, due to the bloodbath, it was gang, or maybe even cartel, related.

On my way out, spotting a small room with a bunch of monitors in it near the front door, well, it seemed like just another act of divine intervention, maybe from the great beyond, a message from a ghost, from Cuddy.

Or maybe, again, it was simply fate. I put the last bullet of the .38 into the mainframe recording device of those cameras, and then smashed it on the marble floor.

I retrieved my car keys from the pocket of the fat dead guy in the foyer, being careful not to leave any shoe prints in the pools of blood.

I went out the front door, walked back to my car, and drove home to the Midwest.

You know, I wasn't scared or frantic. I was calm, at peace. I even stopped at a scenic overlook near Gallup, New Mexico, and watched the sun come up.

29

A Little Peace

Maybe in the next life, the three of us won't ever grow up. Maybe we'll stay young and innocent forever. Maybe we can meet right here someday, atop this mountain, on this rock, and start anew. I don't know what happens when you die, but I'd like to think it's not the end. We keep striving for something in life, so why wouldn't we keep striving for something in death?

I came back to my life a changed man. I left Rachel. A few days after I got back from Arizona and put down a deposit on an apartment in the city, I told her I knew what was going on. I told her I wasn't going to waste my life anymore. She was shocked, dismayed, confused. She pleaded with me to stay. I relished it a bit, even took her to bed. Afterward, when she thought all was back to normal again, allowing me my moment of independence, I started packing my things. She flew into a rage and cried hysterically. Her world had been turned upside down. I remember thinking it was nothing compared to what Holly Karlan went through.

But I'm pleased to say our relationship is much better now than it was when we were together. We talk more. We respect each other.

Elsa took the news with a shrug. "About time," she said. She likes visiting me in the city, staying over on the weekends. We go to shows and museums. She says I'm different now, happier, fun. I'm not such a tool. She talks to me, points out pretty women my age whom I should ask out. We hang out. She wanted to know what happened in Arizona that made me seem so laid back now.

I told her something can happen in an instant that can change you forever, can cause you heartache for the rest of your life. And something can happen in an instant that can bring peace to your soul for the rest of your life. I've experienced both.

Sometimes I think about that, not specifically the events of the past but about how fate has and hasn't played a part in my life. I get up every morning and go to work, come home, and walk the riverfront. I wouldn't say I'm free, but I'm more alive than I've ever been.

As I stated, I do still think about what happened, nearly every day, but not all of it. Not everything. And it doesn't haunt me anymore. There is no blinding guilt.

I came back here, to Arizona, to this mountain, to this rock, the Praying Monk, to say goodbye to my friends and to do something else. On my climb up here I found a dark and narrow crevice, took one long, last look at the .38, and then dropped it into the darkness. I figured it was a fitting resting place, and it was as good a time as any to get rid of the thing.

I haven't heard a word from any cops, not about Cuddy's disappearance or Coach Drago or the bloodbath at Rory's mansion. Not about anything. I read online that Rory lingered in a coma for three or so weeks before succumbing to his severe injuries. I won't lie, that made me feel pretty good. And, yes, I do realize that's not a healthy reaction to such news, but I'm not sure what would even constitute a healthy reaction under the circumstances. I try not to analyze such things. Rory suffered, and that's all that matters. He died an excruciating death. He got what he deserved.

If that's evil, then so be it.

But I'm here to say goodbye—goodbye to my true love, Holly Karlan, and goodbye to my best friend, J. Cuddy.

May the three of us be together again someday, if the fates allow.

www.ingramcontent.com/pod-product-compliance
Lightning Source LLC
Chambersburg PA
CBHW051250250626
47155CB00009B/3240